INVASION OF THE UNDEAD

DEATHSTALKER CHRONICLES BOOK 1

SAMURAI DAN COGLAN

L'OSTE VINEYARD PRESS

Copyright © 2021 by Dan Coglan

All rights reserved.

No part of this book may be reproduced in any form or by any electronic or mechanical means, including information storage and retrieval systems, without written permission from the author, except for the use of brief quotations in a book review.

First paperback edition May 2021

Book Design by Katherine Peragine

ISBN 978-1-7353896-7-7 (Paperback)

ISBN 978-1-7353896-9-1 (eBook)

Published by L'Oste Vineyard Press

www.LosteVineyardPress.com

To Jillian, for believing in a dream.

PROLOGUE

"Get those damn charges set, and let's get out of here," I growled into my mic. Shadows moved around me, and a turbaned face appeared out of the murky darkness. I shot the onrushing insurgent twice and looked around for more.

"Come on, come on, come on," I muttered. "We're past time for evac. Move your slow asses!"

Lt. Rodriquez was suddenly at my side, scowling. "We're doing the best we can, Corporal. Hold on to your hat."

"Charges set, Lieutenant," Stevens called out. "That makes all four; we can blow this popsicle stand!"

"About damn time," I snapped. "There are hostiles everywhere. What the hell is this place, anyway?"

McGavin scoffed. "It's a temple, Brooks. Remember? We had a briefing and everything."

"Screw you," I told him. "This ain't like no temple that I've ever seen. And it smells like a fucking crypt."

"No lie," my buddy, Lance Corporal Jeremy Stevens, chimed in.

"Marines," Rodriquez barked. "Let's go."

I led us back out, the six of us in tight formation. Stevens was on my left flank; Sgt. Bates was on my right, and the Lieutenant was in the middle with the beady-eyed "guide" that the Colonel had stuck us with. McGavin brought up the rear.

Dead bodies were everywhere; our ingress had come with a high body count. I ignored them. Two tours had made me immune to corpses. I had bigger priorities.

There was a commotion in front of us; heard but not seen. Voices cried out in excitement. We froze.

Our position was suddenly hit with massive spotlights. "We've been cut off! Break left!" Rodriquez yelled as gunfire erupted all around us. We returned fire, hot and heavy.

Being in front has its disadvantages. I got hit three times, twice in the chest and once in the leg. My vest took the brunt of the two to the chest, but the leg shot really sucked. I went down but staggered back to my feet and kept fighting.

Stevens took over point; Lt. Rodriquez slid over to his spot and put me in the middle with the guide, who looked scared out of his mind. I didn't blame him.

We raced through the gloom, moving downhill but not having a choice in the matter. McGavin took a round to the lower back and went down. I shouted, and the unit took up positions around our fallen comrade.

We created a semi-circle facing back the way we'd come, weapons up and ready. There wasn't long to wait. The horde was on us quickly, the heavy sound of their AK-47s threatening to overwhelm the sharper cracks of our M-4s.

It was over in less than sixty seconds, and to my amazement, we were still standing. There were bodies all around us, and the air was thick with the smell of cordite. Clouds of smoke from the gunfire obscured our lights even further.

It was like being in hell, I thought, sweeping the area with my carbine. Something flashed in my light, and I swung back.

There was a figure standing at the edge of the light. It couldn't be a friendly, so I shot at it. I missed, and it ducked behind a pile of bodies. The Lieutenant motioned, and Stevens and I went out to get whoever it was.

I'd taken maybe three steps when the figure reappeared, much closer. I could tell it was a man, head and neck wrapped in a shemagh. One arm was holding a bundle, and the other was outstretched toward the ceiling.

His eyes were glowing red. I blinked. His eyes really were glowing; it wasn't goggles or an optical illusion. Glowing or not, I knew what my job was. I put that head with glowing eyes in my sights and prepared to pull the trigger.

Our guide, who'd been useless and paranoid the entire mission, started screaming and babbling in complete gibberish. The only part that I could make out was something about *Manziel* or *manzazu* or some such nonsense, but his outburst caught me off guard, and I missed my shot.

Suddenly there was movement all around us. The bodies of the enemy combatants were stirring. Impossibly, they were staggering to their feet. All around us, corpses were rising from the floor, their eyes shining a baleful crimson.

"What the fuck?" Stevens shouted. "This ain't happening, man."

I put a three-round burst into the chest of the corpse nearest me and blew out his heart. It didn't seem to affect him at all; he just kept shuffling toward me, his arms reaching out. I shot him again, this time doing the Mozambique technique that had been drilled into all Marines. The two shots to the body didn't do anything, but the follow-up round to the head dropped it.

I could hear my unit screaming, cursing, and shooting the reanimated dead bodies all around me. They were coming at us from every direction.

We tightened our circle, trying to cover one another as we changed mags and shifted targets. It didn't matter; they overwhelmed us. There were just too many of them, and we couldn't put them down fast enough.

I watched in horror as my best friend, Jeremy Stevens, was pulled down by a mob of zombies and torn apart. Behind me, Lt. Rodriquez screamed, and then his voice trailed off into a muffled gurgle, and I knew he was gone, too.

My mag ran dry, and I reached for another, determined to keep fighting. My fingers closed on air. I was out. The undead pressed in, their hands clawing for me. I swung the empty rifle like a club, trying to clear a space.

The undead mob pulled the rifle from my hands, so I drew my Colt 1911 handgun. It was a fine weapon, and I was good with it, but it only held eight rounds. Those eight rounds went quickly. When the pistol was empty, all sounds of gunfire ceased.

I was the last of the unit standing. The zombies surrounded me. To my right, two of the obscene things were eating my Sergeant. Behind them, more were tearing our guide to pieces.

I spun to my left and saw what was left of Stevens. Hands fastened onto my vest, and I twisted away. More grabbed hold of my legs, and I went down.

The zombies crowded around me. Behind them, looking on, was the man with the glowing eyes, triumph on his face. He cackled with glee.

In desperation, I felt around for anything to use as a weapon. My hands reached above my head and found the remains of the Lieutenant. His head had been ripped off. My hands shifted lower and found the detonator on his belt for the explosive packages that we'd set.

I yanked it free and held it up. The zombies were all over me, and their leader was looking down at me, sneering.

"Fuck you," I screamed and pushed the button. There was a distant rumble, a pressure wave, and then the world collapsed on me.

CHAPTER 1

I OPENED my eyes to see bright sunshine streaming through a window. To say I was surprised would be an understatement. My last memory was of a stone temple blowing up with me in it.

The thought of the temple led immediately to my unit and what had happened to us. I tried to sit up. Pain lanced through my entire body, and I groaned and lay back on the bed I was in.

A door opened, and a nurse in hospital greens poked her head into the room. She smiled brightly and came bustling in.

"Mr. Brooks, you have your eyes open," she exclaimed, acting for all the world like me opening my eyes was a monumental achievement. Maybe it was; it certainly hurt and required effort.

I tried to answer her, but all I managed was a dry croak. She moved to my bedside and held a Styrofoam cup of water to my face. I sipped from the straw and then tried again.

"Where am I?" I managed to rasp.

"You're safe and sound, Mr. Brooks, here at the hospital. You just sit tight here for a bit; some people want to see you," she told me while plumping my pillows and arranging the sheets.

"Hospital? Where?" I asked. "How long?"

The nurse shook her head. "Don't get yourself worked up, Mr.

Brooks. All your questions will be answered in short order. The doctor will be in soon."

I drifted off then and opened my eyes again when I heard voices. One of them was familiar.

"Colonel LeMasters, sir?" I mumbled.

"Corporal Brooks. It's good to see you awake," a deep voice answered. "Very good."

I focused, and the blurry image standing on my right sharpened into a trim looking man in fatigues who I recognized. "Colonel."

Another man was with him, wearing a white lab coat. I assumed he was a doctor. He checked my pulse, shined a light in my eyes, and generally made a nuisance of himself. I waved him off after he showed no sign of stopping his exam.

"Where am I?" I asked the Colonel. I hurt too much, and my throat was too sore for military protocol. The Colonel didn't seem to mind.

"Corporal, you're Stateside. VA Hospital in Chesapeake. Your hometown, I understand. Mine as well," LeMasters said.

"How?"

The Colonel frowned. "You mean 'how did you get here,' or 'how long have you been here?'"

I nodded. "Both," I managed to croak.

LeMasters glanced at the doc, who shrugged. The Colonel leaned in closer. "Brooks, you've been here for three weeks. You've been in and out of consciousness for the last two days."

Three weeks, I repeated in my head. Three weeks. "What happened?" I asked, not sure that I wanted to hear the answer.

"You were found in the rubble. There was an explosion, and a building collapsed. You were the only survivor from your unit, Corporal. I'm sorry, but the only other person that lived was the guide who was sent with you."

Something about that last sentence bothered me, but I couldn't tell what it was. I was still adjusting to being alive. And back in the States.

"How bad am I?"

LeMasters looked over at the doctor, who stepped up and cleared his throat. He made a show of rechecking his chart and nodding thoughtfully. At length, he looked over the top of the chart at me.

"You have suffered a traumatic brain injury and have been unconscious or semi-conscious for the better part of four weeks. You were shot in the right leg. You were lucky there; the bullet missed both your femur and the femoral artery. There will only be a minimal scar. There was concern about a possible spinal cord injury, but you have demonstrated feeling in all of your extremities, so the consensus is that your back and spine will be fine.

"You have four cracked ribs, which are well on their way to healing, and lastly, you have two broken fingers on your left hand, which have been set and splinted," he continued.

"All in all, now that you have regained consciousness, you are in excellent shape, physically," the doctor concluded, putting a strange emphasis on the "physically."

I looked at the Colonel, who flushed and looked away. "We'll address that later, Brooks," he muttered. He looked uncomfortable, which bothered me. I'd never seen my CO look anything but in charge and positive.

Yawning, I mumbled, "Okay. We'll talk more later, sir. I don't know why I'm so tired if all I've been doing is sleeping for the last month."

The Colonel and doctor faded away, and I floated off. My slumber wasn't entirely peaceful; there were fragmented images of my buddies, and a dark evil place, and yelling and gunshots and... glowing red eyes, boring into my skull.

When I opened my eyes again, the Colonel was in the room, this time with another guy in a lab coat. This guy was looking at me far more critically than the MD had been. I instinctively didn't like this one.

"As I was saying, Colonel LeMasters, I have grave concerns about accepting anything that he says at face value right now. The recordings of his ramblings while in delirium are quite obviously impossible. I advise that we wait before talking to him in detail about what happened," the new guy lectured, sounding very much like a self-important blowhard. Which told me that he was a shrink.

"Talk to me about what?" I asked, making them both jump. I took satisfaction in that. "What recordings?"

LeMasters said, "Don't worry about that, Brooks. We'll get to it in time. I want to introduce you to someone. This is Dr. Sovers. He works here at the VA with returning vets, and he'll be working with you once you're up to it," he explained, waving a hand at the bespectacled doctor.

"Hi doc," I said, to be friendly. Then I did a double-take. "Wait, you said he works with returning vets," I scowled. "What's that mean?"

Dr. Sovers answered. "Mr. Brooks, you were medically discharged from the Marine Corps when they shipped you back to the States. Your second tour was almost up, and it was easier for the Corps and for your recovery to have you discharged.

"The Colonel was able to fast track your benefits package, and since he also has...ah, retired from active duty, he has taken an interest in your rehabilitation," the shrink said.

I watched the Colonel closely as Sovers was speaking, and I read much more than just what the shrink was telling. My former CO didn't look like a man that had chosen retirement amid an armed conflict.

The look on his face matched what my heart felt like. I was no longer a Marine. The loss was palpable. The only feeling of home and of belonging that I'd ever known was gone. I was alone.

That feeling triggered the memory of my team and how they had met their end. I shuddered.

"What about my unit, sir? Were they recovered?" I asked hoarsely.

Colonel LeMasters nodded. "Yes, son, they were—all four of them and several enemy combatants. You boys certainly did the

Marines proud before that explosion took out the building. We'll have a full debrief once you're able, of course, but what happened was pretty clear."

"Sir," I started, not sure how to proceed. "Sir, my unit...we didn't get blown up. I mean, we did, but that's not how they died. We need to talk, sir, privately. Right away," I said, jerking my head to indicate the shrink standing nearby. "Privately," I reiterated.

Sovers snorted and moved closer. "Mr. Brooks, I am in fact in charge of your recovery, and I have military clearance for anything up to and exceeding your unit's activities. There's nothing that you can tell the Colonel that I can't hear."

I looked at LeMasters questioningly. He nodded his expressionless face. As a line animal, I knew exactly what the blank look meant: He didn't like it, but an order was an order.

So I told the truth. The Colonel deserved to hear it, and the shrink didn't matter, at least in my book.

"Sir, we breached the temple and set the charges, just like we were tasked with. On our way out, we were ambushed. We kept formation and looked for a different way out. McGavin was rearguard and got hit in the back, below his vest. We slowed down to pick him up and got overrun," I recited, seeing it all unfold in my head.

"And that's when Lieutenant Rodriquez set off the charges?" LeMasters asked.

"No, sir. We put the raghea...er, insurgents down, sir. We took them all. Then this guy showed up at the edge of the lights. Sir, I know it sounds crazy, but I swear this is the truth. The guy's eyes glowed red, and then the dead guys all started getting up. Their eyes were shining too.

"They killed my unit, sir. I fought until I was out of ammo, and then I found the Louie's detonator and blew up the temple," I finished, knowing just how insane I sounded.

LeMasters frowned. He appeared to be considering what I'd told him.

Dr. Sovers, on the other hand, was shaking his head vigorously.

"This is a mistake. Clearly, Mr. Brooks is not feeling well. We should wait and talk more when he is better rested. The patient needs rest. I'll prescribe something that will help him sleep."

It was my turn to shake my head. "No. I don't need anything to help me sleep. I've slept enough. It's time to get up. I want out of this bed," I announced and tried to get up.

Sovers put his hands on my shoulders and pushed me back on the bed. As weak as I was, I couldn't struggle much. He held me down and clucked at me in disapproval.

"Mr. Brooks, you must rest. Calm yourself. Don't force us to place you in restraints," he said. He tried to make it sound like he'd regret tying me down, but I felt like he'd enjoy nothing more than strapping me to my bed.

I looked at the Colonel for help. He saw the look. "That won't be necessary, doctor. I'm sure that Brooks will rest more comfortably if he's free to move around some. He'll behave, won't you?" He asked, glaring at me.

"Sir, yes, sir," I responded. Once a Marine, always a Marine. It had sounded like an order, so I replied like it was. And I followed that order. I lay back and was compliant.

In my head, though, I was reliving the events in the temple. Long after the Colonel and the shrink left, I lay in the darkness and replayed everything.

CHAPTER 2

IT WAS two full weeks before I saw Sovers again. If he was actually in charge of my rehab, he was doing it from a distance. My days were spent eating anything, everything put in front of me, and going to physical therapy.

The first day doing PT was an exercise in agony. Who knew that lying still in a comfy bed for a month would lead to such muscle atrophy? Other than my physical therapist—Allison expected it and warned me that life would be comprised of hard work, pain, and small victories.

She was right. I couldn't even get out of bed by myself at first. Walking was impossible. Allison had two aides position me to hold rails with my trembling arms and try to support my own weight with my legs. Once I could do that, I tried to drag my feet forward in some semblance of a walk.

It was during one of those sessions that Dr. Sovers dropped by. I was making progress and could almost walk on the treadmill without support. I focused on my task, feeling Allison's eyes on me when I felt another presence.

I tried to turn and look, and of course, fell right on my ass. It hurt my body, but not nearly as much as it did my pride. The therapist shut off the treadmill and checked me out while I sat on my butt and glared at the intruding shrink.

"Mr. Brooks. Hard at it, I see," he observed. It would have been unprofessional of him to smirk, but I swear there were hints of one around his eyes. "Miss Juneau here tells me that you are working quite hard. Just what I'd expect from you."

"Yes, doctor, Chase is working really hard. I'm proud of him," she said, patting my shoulder like I was some prize horse.

"Good to hear. Mr. Brooks, when you're finished with your physical therapy, it's time we had our first session. I'll have an aide bring you down to my office. Plan for one o'clock, okay? That way, you can eat lunch first," he said, checking his watch.

"See you then," he told me and walked out, not bothering to say goodbye to my physical therapist. I scowled after him. Everything about the man rubbed me the wrong way. I had a feeling that "therapy" with him was going to be more like combat than mental health building.

"Chase? Are you okay? You look angry," Allison said, helping me to my feet. "Let's move to the weight machine. We'll work arms and upper body and give your legs a rest for a bit. Then we'll hit the stationary bike.

"Does that sound good to you?" She asked, all polite and concerned. On the whole, I liked her much better than the departed shrink.

I nodded. Trying to get back into shape was imperative. I hated feeling helpless, and right now, I couldn't defend myself against a kindergartner, let alone a grown man. Or an undead one.

For the next half hour, I pushed the free weights around. After that, I rode the bike. Boring, but at least I had Allison for company. Finally, at noon, I suffered the indignity of being helped with a shower, went back to my room, and ate lunch.

At ten minutes until one, two orderlies appeared at my door with a wheelchair. They helped me into the chair, and we set off for the psychiatric wing of the VA. The orderlies didn't speak. Not being big on conversation myself, I didn't mind.

We got out of the elevator on the fifth floor, and I was wheeled into a reception area with a large waiting room. A severe-looking woman sat at a desk beside a locked door. She barely glanced up as I stopped in front of her.

"Yes?" She asked.

"Chase Brooks, to see Dr. Sovers," one of the aides replied.

She flipped through a couple pages on her clipboard and then gestured with her pen at the waiting area. "Wait there. I'll call you when the doctor is ready to see you."

Without another word, the orderlies deposited me in a corner and left. I sat quietly and studied other people waiting. I wasn't impressed; none of them looked even remotely active duty.

You're not exactly in top shape yourself, Corporal, a voice beside me said. I jumped in my chair. There wasn't anyone sitting within ten feet of me. And the voice sounded very familiar.

I frowned and looked around. No one was paying me the slightest bit of attention. I dug a finger into my right ear and wiggled it.

What the hell are you doing, Brooks? Trying to itch your brain? Good luck, the voice commented. I recognized that sarcasm. It was the voice of my former drill instructor, who'd joined our unit when our regular sergeant had been transferred.

"Sergeant Bates?" I asked uncertainly. The sergeant couldn't be here; I watched him die in Afghanistan with the rest of my unit.

A couple of the people nearest to me looked over. They looked nervous. I glared at them. "What?" I growled. They looked away quickly.

Don't bully them, Brooks, just because you're mad. It ain't their fault you're here, Bates snapped. I looked around desperately. There had to be a microphone or something; some trick. Bates was dead.

The woman at the reception desk looked my way. I thought she would tell me to keep it down, but she just pointed at the door with her pen and then went back to work on her computer.

I rolled my way up to the door, still looking around to find where the voice of my deceased drill instructor was coming from. The receptionist pressed a button under her desk, and the door buzzed, indicating that it was unlocked.

I struggled mightily with opening the door, which opened outward. No one helped. Finally getting through the doorway, I entered the psych wing.

Immediately to my right, there was a guard station. Behind a table, staring at a variety of cameras, was a security guard. He was dressed as a Marine, but he didn't look like he'd pass the physical.

He came to his feet as I entered. "Name?" He snapped.

I looked at him. "Brooks. Like you didn't know that. They just buzzed me in." I hated the repetition and stupidity of basic security, and my nerves were already strained from hearing a voice from the grave out in the waiting room.

The guard glared at me. "Don't get smart, boy. It's my job to check and to make sure that anyone coming in is clean. You got anything on you that you shouldn't?"

I glared right back. "I'm wearing hospital clothes and sitting in a damn wheelchair. What the hell do you think I could be carrying, a bazooka?"

"I gotta check you anyway. It's regs," he told me. I wondered how someone like this could have actually passed the qualifications to join the Corps.

He patted me down, which I endured with poor grace. Once he was finished, he made a mark on his clipboard and pointed down the hall.

"First door on the right, Brooks. Knock first, okay? Don't be rude," he lectured me.

"Yes, sir," I saluted and stared at his tape. "Corporal Paxton. Thank you, sir," I told him, careful to pronounce the "sir" so that he knew I was mentally spelling it as "cur." It was an old enlisted man's trick, and if he was really a Marine, he'd know it.

I wheeled myself away before we could exchange further pleasantries. Stopping at the first door, I knocked and then opened it. Inside waited for Dr. Sovers, sitting behind his desk with his fingers steepled in front of him.

"Come on in, Mr. Brooks. Right on time, I see. Good for you," he said. He may not have been deliberately patronizing me, but every shrink that I'd ever met seemed to talk down to everyone.

"I try," I responded, just to be saying something.

"Well, let's jump right in, shall we? We have much to discuss, and we should start with the events that occurred overseas during your last mission, okay? He asked, setting a recorder in the center of his desk and turning it on.

"So tell me, Mr. Brooks, all about your last mission," he said, leaning forward to speak into the recorder.

So I did. I spoke slowly, clearly, and without emotion, reciting the facts like I was reading them off a teleprompter. Dr. Sovers sat back and let me talk without interruption. When I was done, he sat forward again.

"And you actually believe that this happened, correct? Your dead foes magically came back to life and then attacked and killed your unit? And you and you alone survived, after blowing up the temple?," he asked, aiming the questions at me but directing his voice at the recorder.

"No shit. Why would I say it if I didn't believe it?" I snapped. "I'm not crazy," I added defensively. The incident in the waiting room flashed across my mind, but I ignored it. "It couldn't have happened, but it did, doc," I insisted.

"It couldn't have happened, and therefore it didn't, you mean," Sovers corrected. "The first step in your recovery must be that we stay grounded in reality, Mr. Brooks. We will go on this journey together, but we will do much better if we start by staying within the boundaries of what IS, as compared to what IS NOT," he pontificated. I don't even think he talked to me; he was lost expounding to the cosmos—the jerk.

"Whatever," I muttered. "I saw what I saw."

"You probably believe that, currently, Mr. Brooks. It isn't unusual for the mind to create an alternate reality to explain things that are too painful for a person to accept. Events unfolded during your mission that you were incapable of preventing, which is how your brain is dealing with it. We'll fix it, I promise," he smiled.

I resisted the urge to test my physical recovery by coming out of the wheelchair and over his desk. It wouldn't help my situation. So I sat and simply stared at him.

"Well, Mr. Brooks, if we're done talking for today, we can call this a wrap," he said and shut off the recorder. "We'll meet again in two days and see if we can make more progress. In the meantime, I suggest that you think about what you think you saw and try to acknowledge the impossibility of it. It will help speed your recovery. Thank you," Sovers finished and turned away from me.

I wheeled myself back down the hallway to the openly hostile Sgt. Paxton. He sneered at me when he held the door open, and I returned the favor with a single-digit salute as I went by. All in all, the whole visit went about the way I thought it would.

CHAPTER 3

THE NEXT DAY I got a visit from Colonel LeMasters. He came in and sat down at the edge of my bed, like a family member rather than the commanding officer of an elite military unit.

"Colonel, sir," I said, and tried to sit up straighter in the bed.

"Good morning, Brooks. How are you doing?" He asked, looking at me intently.

"Fine, sir. Better every day," I told him.

He nodded. "I heard that your first therapy session was...challenging. That you are still insisting that your unit was killed by dead soldiers and not by the explosion that you set off."

I stared. I could see now where things were going. I was being blamed for killing the men that were the closest friends that I'd ever had in my life. And that I had not only failed them but the Marine Corps as well.

The Colonel must have read all that on my face. He stood up and squared his chin. "Corporal, did you kill your unit?" He asked, his voice chillingly formal.

I scowled. "No. No, sir, I did not," I snapped back.

"Did you abandon them in their hour of need, Corporal?"

"No. No, sir. Never. I would have died first," I declared.

"Oorah," the Colonel grunted.

"Oorah!" I shouted back.

Colonel LeMasters relaxed his posture and sat down in a chair. "I believe you, Brooks. At least, I believe that you didn't kill your men or lead them to their deaths. Beyond that, let's say that I retain a high level of ambivalence."

"Ambivalence, sir? I'm just a grunt, sir. If I knew big words, I would have been an officer," I told him. He cracked a grin.

"Brooks, you are an insolent son of a bitch; I'll give you that," he said.

I cocked an eyebrow. "Insolent?"

"Alright, enough, Brooks. You're not as dumb as you let on. I get it; it's a tactical advantage to make others view you as less competent than you really are. Don't pull that shit on me; I'm on your side."

"Then tell me what's going on, sir," I demanded. "Why are you even here if you retired, sir?"

LeMasters looked at me. "Who said I was retired? I was reassigned from combat duty to work Stateside. I'm now in charge of this hospital. I'm a pencil pusher," he said, his tone self-mocking.

"But Sovers said..." I started. He held up a hand to stop me.

"Dr. Sovers said it wrong, Brooks. He's a shrink, not a Marine. He's also new here, came over from some Pentagon station. I don't know anything about him, but top brass favors him. Stay on his good side, Marine," he warned.

I made a sour face. "Not much chance of that," I told him. I sat up higher in the bed. "Sir? What happened over there? I mean, why did we hit that temple anyway?"

LeMasters hesitated. "I can only tell you what you're cleared to know, son. And some rumors from the village.

"We had intel that insurgents were arming and doing ops out of that temple. The high priest or whatever was some sort of petty dictator in the area, demanding money and women, and even infants for sacrifice. It'd been that way for years before the U.S. ever got involved.

"Anyway, we got solid intel that a hit was going to happen at our FOB and that they were coming from the tunnels under the temple. So I tasked a small squad to take out the temple, hopefully with the weapons and priest in the temple when it went up.

"I sent a guide, somebody in the village that knew his way around underground and could speak the language if you guys got in a tight spot.

"The rest you know," he concluded. "The temple did get blown up, thanks to you, and the priest got taken out. But your unit paid the price. Only you and the guide got out," he added, shaking his head.

"Command viewed the op as a mistake, and I got pulled and sent here to finish out my 30," LeMasters grimaced. "Desk jockey at this place."

"Sir," I interrupted him before he could complain more about his unfortunate lot. "Sir, there's a problem with that story. The guide was not only no help at all, but he didn't make it, either. I saw him literally get his arms ripped off. He was torn apart. He had to be dead."

LeMasters frowned. "Son, you must be mistaken. Abdul-Rayef is here. He was granted citizenship as an apology from our government. I personally brought him to Chesapeake. He was on my flight."

"Can't be," I breathed. I saw him die, I told myself.

Maybe you're wrong. You have been wrong about a lot in your life, Sergeant Bates intruded into my thoughts.

I looked around, startled. "Sir? Did you say something?" I asked the Colonel.

"Yes. I said that he was on my flight," LeMasters repeated.

"Not that," I said, waving my hand at him in annoyance. What the hell is going on, I wondered.

LeMasters looked at me strangely. "Are you okay, Brooks?"

"Yeah, I'm fine," I muttered. A derisive snicker met that pronouncement. I was looking right at the Colonel, and I knew that he hadn't done it.

This time I refused to look around. I ignored whatever voice that was. Maybe it would go away.

"Sorry, sir, I think I'm just tired," I lied. I didn't want the Colonel to think that I was losing my mind.

He stood and smiled. "Sure. Get some rest, Brooks. I'll be in to check on you soon," he told me and left quietly.

After I was confident that he was gone and not listening at the door, I got up and searched my room. I didn't find any hidden mics or cameras or anything. Sitting back on the edge of my bed, I said, "Whoever you are, you're not funny. Come on out."

Nothing. No one stepped out from the shadows, and no voice answered me. I tried it again. "Look, I know the sergeant is dead. So whoever you are, you're mimicking a dead man."

I sat in silence. "Huh, coward. Big shock. C'mon, answer me," I implored. "I need someone to talk to." Still nothing. I got up off of the bed and waved my arms around.

"Hey, chickenshit, I'm right here. Talk to me," I demanded.

"Chase?" A quiet voice called.

I spun and faced the door. It was open a crack, and the worried face of Allison Juneau peered into the room. My face flushed as I realized that she'd heard me. And probably seen me, talking to the room and making stupid hand gestures in the air.

"Yeah, what?" I asked sourly, looking at the floor in shame.

"It's time for your physical therapy appointment. I thought that I'd come to get you myself. Is now not a good time?" She asked nervously. "I can give you a few minutes to, ah, collect yourself if you need."

"No, I'm fine," I said, glaring around the room in anger. "Let's go," I told her, pulling open the door and marching out past her.

"Chase? I brought a wheelchair for you," she called after me.

I kept going. "I don't need it. I feel fine."

She hurried after me, her nursing crocs slapping on the tiled floor. I beat her to the elevator and pushed the button. I felt pretty good about beating her, even if it was just a short walk.

We made it the rest of the way to physical therapy without speaking. She looked like she wanted to talk, but I just glared straight ahead and kept my jaw clenched. At least there weren't any other unwanted voices on the trip.

CHAPTER 4

SHORTLY AFTER MY disastrous meeting with Dr. Sovers, I had an actual visitor. I was on the floor beside my bed, pumping out extra pushups, when there was a hesitant tap on my door. I got to my feet, straightened my hospital robe as best I could, and called, "It's open."

The door swung inward, and a wizened face peered around it at me. When I was spotted, the face crinkled up into something like a smile, and an old man edged his way into my room.

"Good to see you up and around, boy," Bill greeted me. "Last time I stopped, you were out like a light."

"Yeah," I grunted. "Sorry to inconvenience you."

"Smartass," he grumped. "I should just leave." He turned as if to walk back out.

"Hey, don't go. Help me eat my extra pudding," I offered, knowing that he'd turn around. True enough, he stopped in the doorway. The old guy, who was the closest thing that I'd ever had to a father, turned around with a grin.

"Forget that shit, I brought you something," he enthused, holding up a bag. "Close the door," he told me, even though he was standing right next to it. I smirked and stepped over beside him and swung it shut.

Bill walked up to my bed, looked around furtively, and then dumped the contents of his bag onto the mattress. It was a plastic box, roughly fifteen inches long, ten inches high, and four or five inches deep. I recognized what it was.

"Bill Freeman, you brought a fucking gun into the hospital? Are you nuts?" I asked, looking around, just as he had not a minute earlier. He laughed.

"Well, don't just stand there wetting your pants, boy, open it up," he instructed.

I popped the two tabs along the bottom edge and opened the case. Resting inside was a beautiful 1911 style handgun, all black. I whistled and reached in to pick it up. The old man reached past me and snatched it up.

"Look at this," he breathed, turning it around in his hands. "See that nice, even black finish? Ionbond coating. Almost impossible to scratch. I know you got big hands and always complained about your military issue 1911 only having eight rounds, so I got you a double stack! See," he turned the butt toward me and took his bottom hand off of the gun.

"Hmm...is it still a 1911, then?" I asked and tried to take it from him.

"Technically, it's a 2011," he informed me, pivoting away so that I couldn't grab it. "Commander sized, so it's got full grips, but only a four and a quarter-inch barrel. You'll be able to draw it faster. Holds fourteen rounds, has Trijicon night sights; it's perfect!"

"Well, if it's so perfect, let me see it," I scowled, trying again to grab the gun. Bill held it away, like a child keeping a favorite toy for himself.

"Here's the best part. Look at this," he wheezed, turning it sideways. "Check out the slide engraving. It says 'Recon.' Just like your unit," he said.

I looked. The slide's right side did indeed have the word *Recon* on it, under a skull and wings logo. "What the hell, did Para start up again? I thought they got bought out and closed."

Bill laughed with delight. "Oh, they're still closed up. Remington bought them. But I got this when they first came out, before they got bought out, and set it aside for you. Check it out," he said, finally handing me the gun.

I took the handgun and swept it up, extending it out and sighting down the slide. It had a marvelous balance. The sights were easy to pick up, and the double-stack grips fit my mitts like it was designed just for them.

I checked it to make sure it was empty and then pulled the trigger. It clicked, the hammer breaking easy and crisp. Overall it was the best weapon that I'd ever seen, much less handled. "This is sweet," I mumbled.

"You damn skippy," Bill agreed. "Here, put it away; I hear somebody coming," he said, holding the open case and gesturing.

"You were nuts to bring that in here," I told him, putting the glistening gun back into its case and snapping it shut. "But I'm glad you did."

Bill looked at me. "You matter, boy. You get well, and then come pay me for this damn thing. All right?"

There was another light knock on my door. It was my night for company. Before I could answer, the door swung in, and Allison Juneau swept into the room.

"Chase, I was wondering if you wanted to get some late-night supper at the cafeteria..." she said, trailing off in embarrassment as she saw that I wasn't alone. "Oh, sorry. I was just, um," she stammered.

I had no idea why she was so red-faced, but Bill was looking from her to me and cackling with merriment. I glared at him. It seemed to have no effect on him.

"Well, I can see that you're in good hands, boy, so I'll go now. You just keep getting better, okay?" He said.

"Yeah, whatever," I told him. "Bill, this is my physical therapist, Allison. Allison, this old senile grump is Bill Freeman. He runs a gun shop that I hung out at a lot as a kid."

Bill extended his hand, which Allison took. "Nice to meet you," she said. "I was just checking in on Chase, I mean Mr. Brooks, since I was here at the hospital late tonight."

"I see," Bill smiled. "Well, I'm on my way home. I don't stay out late anymore. You kids have fun," he said, winking at me. Allison flushed and looked away. I took the opportunity to flip him the bird. The old coot just laughed and walked off.

Allison and I walked to the cafeteria in awkward silence. The late-night menu was pretty limited, but the food was food. I grabbed two hamburgers and two orders of fries and put them on the counter next to Allison's salad. She paid, and we sat down in a booth.

"Well," she started. "How are you doing? I mean, other than your physical recovery, I know all about that. Had any other visitors or anything fun like that?"

I snorted. "Fun. Not hardly. No fun. And no other visitors. Just Bill. Why?"

She smiled sadly. "That's too bad. You should have company, it helps a lot. No other visitors? What about your other therapy? With Dr. Sovers?"

I growled through a mouthful of hamburger. "That asshole. He assigned me to group therapy. I told him I didn't want to go. Idiot."

She leaned forward. "What happened?"

I grimaced. "About what you'd expect. After two sessions, I got uninvited. Apparently, I upset the other patients. Sovers told me that I set their recoveries back at least six months. So now I don't have to go.

"Hell," I said through another bite. "I don't even have to wait in line when I go for my appointments. I'm 'unsettling' to the other vets in the waiting room, according to the troll they have for a receptionist."

Allison shook her head. "Chase, you should try to get along with those people. They're vital to your recovery and getting on with your life."

"Getting on with my life? Lady, my life ended in an explosion in

Afghanistan, with my unit," I scowled. "This is just some form of hell that I ended up in."

She was hurt, I could tell. She stiffened like she'd just seen something ugly crawling in her salad. I'd screwed up. It was just hard to give a damn. My team was gone. And they weren't coming back. What else mattered?

She's hot, a voice said. I jumped and looked around. In the process, I knocked over the salt shaker. Allison flinched when I jumped and looked at me strangely.

"Are you okay?" She asked, somewhat coldly.

"Did you hear...never mind," I mumbled. I recognized the voice, and there was no way she could have heard it. Jeremy Stevens was dead. Which meant that I shouldn't have heard it, either.

At that moment, I saw Colonel LeMasters walk into the cafeteria. What the head honcho was doing here at 8:30 at night was a mystery. I waved a hand, and he noticed and came over briskly.

"Brooks," he nodded, his eyes searching the room. He didn't seem to notice Allison.

"Colonel, sir," I replied. "This is my physical therapist, Allison Juneau," I added. The Colonel gave a distracted wave and kept looking around.

"Sir? Anything wrong? Need help with anything?" I asked.

He jerked his attention back to our table and took a deep breath. "No, thanks, Brooks. We have a missing child. Injured Marine, going through rehab, like you are. His wife and their four-month-old son came in this afternoon to visit. She stepped out to use the restroom for a minute, and when she returned, the baby was gone. We're looking."

Allison looked concerned. "Don't we have cameras on all the floors?"

The Colonel looked around the room again quickly and then leaned in closer. "Our entire camera system went down earlier this afternoon. Talk about worst-case scenario coincidence."

I frowned, and LeMasters cut me off before I could start. "I know, son, we're Marines; we don't believe in coincidences. Noted. I need to keep moving. Keep your eyes peeled, Brooks, and Miss, ah, Juneau," he said and walked off.

When he left, we both bolted down our food and joined the search. We spent almost three hours going over every inch of space in the hospital that was open, along with dozens of staffers and other volunteers, and the police. We didn't find a single clue.

Allison insisted on walking me back to my room rather than letting me walk her to her car. It was the perfect ending to a totally awkward and weird evening. I hesitated to call it a date.

At one a.m. I shut the TV off and tried to sleep. I lay in the darkness and stared at the ceiling, seeing my unit being overrun with dead bodies that moved with purpose and malice. Finally, somewhere around three thirty in the morning, I drifted into an uneasy slumber.

CHAPTER 5

A HARSH SOUND woke me out of an uneasy sleep. It came from outside of my room, at the nurses' station. There was an outcry, cut off suddenly, ending with a crunching sound.

I sat up, listening. My brain told me that I imagined things, and it was just part of a vivid dream. My brain said all of that; my gut told me something entirely different. I felt the rush of adrenaline hit my system and the hot flush on my cheeks.

The lights out in the bay went out. My room was already dark, with the door closed and the shades drawn, but the light had trickled in through the cracks. No more. My room was now pitch black.

I got out of bed and worked my way to the door, stubbing my toe on the bedside tray on wheels. I swore under my breath at the pain and the noise.

A quiet voice in my head hissed at me to be quiet, but I ignored it. There wasn't time to deal with imaginary voices.

Just as I put my hand on the door handle, it turned; someone was opening my door from outside. I let go and shifted to the side, flattening myself against the wall away from where the door would swing.

The door burst open, and two figures rushed into the room past me. They moved quickly but with odd movements, stiff and uncoordinated. They reached my bed and discovered that it was empty.

The two figures turned around to see where I was, and my heart stopped. They had red glowing eyes. They saw me and came at me with arms outstretched.

I blinked my eyes, trying to clear away what had to be a dream. When I opened them, I still saw the figures, but now they were right on top of me.

The one on the left grabbed me by my shoulders and leaned in to tear into my throat. The one on the right grabbed my hips and went for my stomach, mouth open wide.

The physical contact broke my paralysis; it proved that they were real and that I wasn't dreaming. Before the one on the left could rip out my jugular, I swept both my arms around in a counterclockwise move that cleared its hands from my shoulders and pushed its head further left and away from me.

At the end of the circular sweep, I dropped my right elbow straight down onto the lower figure's head while at the same time pulling my right leg back, giving me extra force on the strike and moving that leg out of the way. The figure went down to its knees.

They were close enough, and my eyes had adjusted to the darkness enough to see that the figures were two dead men, wearing the same hospital "johnnies" that I had on.

The zombie that I'd swept away came back at me immediately. It tried to grab my shoulders again, but I thwarted it with a left uppercut to its chin. I heard teeth click together and break. I put both hands on its chest and shoved it further away from me.

The one on its knees tried to get up, but I swung around and sat on it like it was a horse. Pushing it back down onto all fours, I leaned over and stuck my fingers into its eye sockets and pulled back, lifting its head. It groaned, an obscene sound that made me cringe.

I forced myself to finish the move despite my revulsion. Shifting from the eye sockets to its neck, I put it in a rear naked choke and then wrenched its head around until I heard a sharp crack. The zombie went limp, and I let go. It collapsed to the floor, the red eyes going dark.

The one that I'd pushed away twice came at me again. They weren't speedy, but they were persistent. Before it could reach me, I thrust out with my right leg in a front kick. I kicked the zombie in the chest, and it grabbed my foot with both hands. This one was faster than I'd given it credit for.

It attempted to raise my bare foot up to its mouth. I resisted by bending my knee, which brought us closer together. I grabbed its head with both hands and gave it a vicious head butt. I heard a bone crunch, but the thing didn't register pain.

Letting go of my leg, the undead thing grabbed my head, mimicking the same hold that I had on it. Instead of trying to pull me into a head butt, though, it yanked upward. The zombie was trying to tear my damn head off!

Images of Lt. Rodriquez flashed through my mind as I struggled with my foe. No way was I going out like that. I dropped my center, ducked my head, and drove my right shoulder into the thing's chest, breaking its grip on my head.

I continued to push, tackling it to the ground. Its cold hands flailed, battering my face and ribs. My hands found its throat. I overlapped my thumbs and shoved down, fracturing its larynx.

What would have been fatal to a living, breathing, human being had absolutely no effect on the undead creature. It kept up its assault, hitting me over and over again. My still-healing ribs were starting to give way, and each strike hurt more than the one before.

In desperation and anger, I raised the zombie's head up off of the floor and then slammed it back into the tiles that made up the floor. I did it again. And again. The zombie ceased its attacks as it lost control over its arms.

I slammed its head down until there was an ugly crunching sound, and blood and brain matter splattered across the floor of my room. I stopped. The zombie was sprawled under me, unmoving.

The red glow had faded from its eyes, and it just looked like a violently abused dead body.

Chest heaving from the exertion, I got to my feet. My hands were shaking from adrenaline, and my legs were trembling. I staggered over and turned on the light. My room was a disaster.

I leaned over, taking deep breaths. Loud voices came from down the hall, and someone turned on the lights to the bay. There was a scream, followed by rushing footsteps. My area of the hospital filled up fast with people, all shouting conflicting orders, asking questions, and running around in circles.

Two nurses guided me to a chair in an empty patient room adjacent to my own. "Stay here. Someone will be in to talk to you soon," one instructed as they ran back out. I sat and watched the frenzy.

Good luck sorting this shit out. I heard Bates comment sourly. I had no reply.

CHAPTER 6

"You're not making any sense!" The cop exclaimed, slamming his hand down on the table. I didn't jump; better, louder men than he was had yelled things at me.

"I didn't say it made sense. I said it was what happened," I told him. "I went to bed late, as usual. I heard a noise and went to see what it was, and those two dead men attacked me. I put them down, and then the cavalry showed up, late as usual.

"Now I get to deal with you," I finished, waving a hand at him and his partner. "Are we done?"

The first cop flushed. "Not by a long shot, buddy. We've got three bodies, all killed similarly, and you, bruised and your hands covered in blood and cranial fluid."

"Yeah, doesn't look good for you, does it?" The second cop asked, leaning over me with a sarcastic look. "A returning vet with PTSD goes berserk and kills his nurse. Not good at all."

I looked up at him. "And then killed two men who were already dead? Is that right? How the hell does that work?"

The two looked at each other. "What do you mean, already dead?" The first asked, looking back at me with a blank expression.

"I heard them talking before you put me in this conference room. The two stiffs were DOAs from the morgue. You already knew that, don't play dumb. What do you think; that I dressed two dead bodies in the morgue, dragged them up here, killed a nurse with one of their sets of hands, and then killed them a second time?" I shook my head. "You guys are idiots."

The standing one glared at me. "Watch it, punk. I bet we can make a homicide charge stick, don't you, Donnie?," he asked his partner.

"Probably. If he doesn't change his attitude," Donnie replied. "We can at least give him an obstruction charge."

Whatever my brilliant reply was going to be got interrupted. Colonel LeMasters threw open the door and stormed into the conference room. He nodded at me and turned to face the two detectives.

"So what's the story, gentlemen? Any idea as to why my nurse was killed and what those two bodies were doing up here? I want answers, and I want them now," he demanded.

Donnie snapped his notebook closed and looked up at him. "No. But when we do, you'll be the first to know, Colonel. Right now, we're interviewing witnesses. Uncooperative ones, at that," he grumped, glaring over at me. "We'll be back. Don't leave town," he warned me.

The two left, and the Colonel sat down opposite me at the table. He rubbed a hand across his eyes and took a deep breath. "What a night. Probably for you, too, huh?" He said.

I nodded.

"So, Brooks, what the hell happened? How did we go from a missing baby to this shit, all in one night?" He wanted to know.

"No idea, sir. I was asleep, and I woke up when the nurse was attacked. Then the two zombies came into my room and attacked me. That's all I know," I told him.

LeMasters shook his head. "They can't have been zombies, Brooks. Dead people do not just get up and walk around, and we both know that. They must have been falsely identified as deceased and woke up in the morgue and came up for some reason, breaking into my office and then coming here and assaulting the nurse and then you."

"Colonel, what have I been trying to tell you? My unit was killed by these things, and now they're here. There's no way they were mistaken for dead and just 'woke up,' sir. This shit is real," I snapped.

I thought about what he'd just said. "Wait. You said they went to your office? How do you know that?"

"My office was broken into tonight. They left the place a mess. One of them spilled ink from my desk onto the floor and tracked it out," he said. He saw my look and waved a hand. "My father used an old quill pen to sign important documents, and he left it to me when he passed."

I shook my head. "It's not that, sir. These things are moving with a purpose. They went after you first and then came to get me. Don't you see what that means?"

"What?"

"It has to be related to what happened overseas, sir. That temple," I told him. "They want to punish us for blowing it up."

LeMasters snorted. "Seriously? They're all dead, Brooks. We've already been punished for that; I got kicked back Stateside to push papers here, and you're out of the Corps. There's no supernatural force after us, young man."

"But sir," I tried. He cut me off.

"Look, Brooks, I sympathize, and I know you've had a rough time. I'm on your side, you know that. And you don't need to worry about those two cops; they were just busting your chops. They know you didn't kill the nurse.

"We'll get you assigned to a new room for the night. In the morning, you're due to be discharged. Your doctor and physical therapist have signed off on it. You'll just need to continue seeing Doctor Sovers weekly.

"Now," he said, climbing back to his feet. "Now I have to get back to cleaning up this mess. Good night, Brooks. We'll talk again soon. We Recon guys have to stick together."

Once he was gone, a nurse came in and escorted me to a new room; one without zombie brains scattered all over the floor. I didn't feel any safer. My enemies were not only real, but they had crossed the ocean to come after me. And no one believed me.

CHAPTER 7

COLONEL LEMASTERS WAS as good as his word. I was released the next morning. I spent my first day setting up my new place. I'd rented half of a furnished duplex in a decent part of town, quiet and out of the way.

Before buying provisions, I stopped at Freeman Lock and Alarm to see Bill and pay for my Para Black Ops Recon and ammo. He talked me into a rifle as well. I didn't put up much of an argument; I'd been planning on buying a cheap AR-15 anyway.

I got funny looks on the bus, riding with a big black shopping bag wrapped around a gun case. I didn't mind being stared at. Being 6'5" and 250 pounds, I was used to getting stared at. Riding the damn bus irritated me. I needed wheels.

After stowing my new DPMS rifle in a closet, I loaded my Para with jacketed hollow points, stuck it in my new in-the-waistband holster, and headed out to buy groceries. Lacking wheels, I had to hoof it. The nearest grocery store, according to my smartphone, was a mile away. Good exercise.

I walked to the end of my driveway and looked around, checking my six, as always. Everything looked fine; all I saw was an older, kinda battered pickup parked at the end of the lane, with a guy sitting in it, talking on his phone.

I walked past him, nodding as I went by. He ignored me. I was used to that and didn't mind. As long as his eyes weren't glowing red, I told myself.

Twenty minutes later, I found the little strip mall with a Kroger's at one end that my phone had insisted was there. I bought as many microwavable meals as I could carry, along with basic staples like peanut butter and bread.

Stepping out of the store with both arms loaded down with groceries, I noticed that walking around like this made me really vulnerable. There was no way to react quickly, and there was a zero chance of drawing my firearm with both hands tied up.

The walk home was twenty minutes of intense stress. My skin crawled, and I felt eyes on me the entire way back. I rubbernecked like a tourist visiting the Vatican. The only thing I saw was a couple of teenagers walking away from the old pickup at the end of my lane, giggling and stuffing their hands into their pockets when they saw me.

I made it inside and dropped the bags on the table. I took a deep breath and let it out. My hands were shaking. Relax, I told myself. Stop being such a pansy. You're fine. I made a vow to never be vulnerable again.

Some tough Marine, I heard Bates sneer. *Scared of being outside in broad daylight.*

Screw you, I retorted. I have a reason. And you know it. You were there, I told him.

There was no answer. Apparently, he knew I was right. It occurred to me that I was not only hearing voices, but I had started answering them. Maybe I *was* crazy.

Dude, you've always been crazy. Ain't nuthin' changed, Stevens laughed.

I jumped despite myself. "Where the hell are you?" I asked quietly. I already knew there was no one in my house.

With you, Stevens answered. *Always.*

"Like that's helpful," I growled. I walked into my small but efficient bathroom and stared into the mirror. Angry blue eyes stared back at me. I looked deeper.

There's nothing in there, Brooks. I told you that back in basic, Sgt. Bates told me.

I shook my head. I had been staring right at my reflection when I heard Bates' voice. Nothing moved or changed, either in my face or in my surroundings. The voices had to be coming from inside my head.

Intellectually, I had known that from the beginning. I just hadn't wanted to admit it. Now I had to. The voices were only in my head, and I was hallucinating.

Hey, at least there's something in your head, McGavin piled on. *The Sarge was wrong about that*, he cackled. McGavin had always been a jerk.

That's enough, I told them. *Ease off. I have enough to deal with.*

Brooks, you don't get to decide when is enough. A Marine takes everything thrown at him and overcomes. But then, you were a sorry Marine, weren't you? Bates yelled, in full drill instructor voice.

"Damn it, it was bad enough when you got reassigned to my unit in Afghanistan, and I had to put up with you. Do you have to be in my head now?" I demanded. My drill instructor had hated me, and by the end of basic training, it was very mutual. It was one of life's great ironies that he'd transferred to my unit during my second tour.

You need me, Bates growled, still at full volume.

"We'll see," I whispered. "We'll see what Sovers thinks of you being here," I told them. There had to be some pill or shot I could take to get rid of them. It would be worth putting up with the overbearing psychiatrist to be free of these voices.

So the next day, I went into the VA for my appointment with Doctor Sovers to tell him about my former unit being in my head. I almost looked forward to meeting with him.

In keeping with my vow concerning being vulnerable, I took both my

Para and an Emerson CQC folding knife. It wasn't easy hiding a double-stack handgun, but I wore the baggiest T-shirt that I owned and made sure to keep my arm tucked against my side to minimize my "print."

I walked right through the waiting room like usual, nodding at the receptionist when she frowned at seeing me and waved me through the door. It wasn't until I stopped at the guard's desk that it occurred to me that I'd brought a loaded weapon into a hospital. The odds were that they wouldn't be thrilled.

"What the hell is that?" Paxton cried, patting me down. "Hold still, damn you," he warned, reaching in and taking out my gun.

"You're not supposed to have this, you nut job," he exclaimed. "This is the psych wing, Brooks. I don't even get to carry here. You stepped in it this time, pal," he said, picking up his phone. He called the security office, giving them the VA's version of a 911, and then called Sovers.

The doc beat the security pukes to the desk, where Paxton was keeping me under guard. Which meant that the jerk was standing over me, glaring, while I sat quietly in the chair that he'd given me.

"Mr. Brooks, what's going on?" Sovers asked, looking at me sternly. I shrugged.

"Dr. Sovers, he brought a loaded gun to the clinic," Paxton blabbed, holding up my Para.

"I see," the shrink said and gave me a serious but thoughtful look. "Mr. Brooks, did you bring that firearm for me? Or perhaps for Corporal Paxton?"

"No," I told him.

"Then why do you have it?" He wanted to know.

"Last time I was here, I was attacked. I was without a weapon. That's not going to happen again," I told him.

Sovers frowned at me. "Not here, you weren't. And you know that incident is still under review, Mr. Brooks. We don't know what happened or why yet. Don't you feel that this is an overreaction?"

I looked straight ahead. "No."

"Do you have any other weapons on you, Mr. Brooks?" Sovers wanted to know.

"Ask him. He's supposed to know," I inclined my head at Paxton.

The security guard flushed. "I didn't get to finish my pat-down, sir. I found the gun and called for backup and then informed you, sir."

Sovers looked at him for a long moment. "I see," he said and then looked at me again. "Well?" He asked, with an eyebrow raised.

I reached into my boot and pulled out the folder. Paxton swore and snatched it out of my hand. I kept my expression neutral.

The locked door to the waiting room opened, and three more guards rushed in, all slightly out of breath. They must have been far away when the call had come in. That or they weren't in excellent shape. I glanced at their beltlines and decided to reserve judgment.

After some jawing back and forth, the guards calmed down, Paxton locked my offending weapons into a safe, and I followed Sovers down the hall to his office. Instead of sitting at his desk, he put me on a small couch and took a chair facing me.

It seemed less formal, but at the same time, reinforced patient versus doctor roles. I didn't like it. I twitched a little, shifting restlessly.

"A little uncomfortable, Mr. Brooks? Is it the lack of weapons? Do you feel vulnerable here, with me?" Sovers asked. He took out his recorder, turned it on, and set it on the table next to him.

"No. Of course not," I answered, through clenched teeth. I knew any other answer would be counted against me.

"That's good, Mr. Brooks. We want this to be a comfortable place, a safe place for us to work through issues and concerns, don't we?" he asked.

I hated having to answer questions that weren't really questions. They were just ploys to get me to agree with everything that he said, like a salesman with his pitch. So I sat and didn't answer.

"Mr. Brooks, I asked you a question," Sovers prodded.

I sighed. "No, doc, you didn't. Not really. If we're gonna do this, can we at least talk like adults?"

"We are adults, Mr. Brooks. I don't understand your problem. Can you tell me more?"

"Don't shrink me. I don't want to answer inane, pointless questions. If we're going to talk, fine, let's talk. But real. Not Psych 101 bullshit," I growled. I think I offended him.

"Now look here, Mr. Brooks. This isn't 'bullshit,' as you call it. It is a process and an important one. You were released from this hospital, but your continued freedom is mostly dependent on how our sessions go.

"To be candid, Mr. Brooks, I recommended against you being released, especially with what happened here your last evening of residence. Colonel LeMasters overruled me and went against my recommendation, but it is possible to have you brought back here if conditions warrant," he told me.

"You bringing a loaded weapon onto the premises is a bad sign, frankly, and I will be discussing it with the Colonel directly. In the meantime," he continued, "is there anything that you would like to discuss?"

I had wanted to discuss the voices in my head, but after that little speech, I knew that there was no way I was going to bring *that* up. Sovers would have me in a bed, pumped full of drugs, and totally unable to defend myself.

I needed to give this man zero ammunition, I realized. For the rest of the appointment, I offered nothing of my own volition and made only brief, to-the-point answers to his direct questions. Battle lines had been drawn.

CHAPTER 8

I STORMED out of the VA, ready to tear someone limb from limb. Sovers had basically threatened to have me locked up as soon as he could contrive a reason, and my rabbi, Colonel LeMasters, had refused to see me, citing administrative duties.

To top it off, that prick security geek, Paxton, had tried to refuse to return my weapons. We'd almost come to blows over it. I stopped when I realized that Sovers baited me, trying to get me to punch the creep and then get admitted against my will. I changed tactics and kissed ass instead, and finally managed to get my handgun and knife back.

After stopping at Freeman Lock and Alarm to order a red dot sight for my new AR-15 and buy a couple more backup weapons to add to my arsenal, I grabbed lunch and caught a damn bus home.

I got dropped off two blocks from my lane, still fuming. I stomped my way with my head down, barely registering the old pickup parked once again at the curb.

"Hey. Hey, man," a voice called—a real voice, not one in my head. I looked up and saw the guy leaning against his truck. "Buddy, you want to party, man?"

"Get lost," I said and kept walking.

"Fuck you, man, you ain't got to be rude," the man snapped back, pushing away from the truck. "No cause, fucker. This is my street, and you need to show respect."

That stopped me. Respect, I asked myself. Not likely. I knew he was a drug dealer and made his living off of getting kids hooked on toxic shit. I turned around slowly and walked back to him. Setting down my bags, I stepped up close.

"What, you a big bad motherfucker, gonna put me in my place?" He asked, tilting his head to the side, staring up at me. "You big, bro; don't make you bad," he added, flipping open a knife.

I knocked it out of his hand with my left and hit him square on the jaw with my right hand, dropping him to the ground. He stayed down for a while, rubbing his jaw and looking at me.

"You crazy, man. You know who I work for?" He asked, spitting blood on the ground at my feet. "Nobody messes with us. You fucked up big-time."

I reached down and grabbed the gang member's shirt, and hoisted him back to his feet. "I don't care who you work for, asshole. There will be no drugs sold on this street—period. Take it down the road," I told him and shoved him back a couple of steps.

He didn't take it well. I knew that because he drew a gun and pointed it at me. It was an old revolver, a Smith & Wesson Model 10. He cocked it and aimed right at my face.

"What, you gonna shoot me in broad daylight?" I asked him. "How stupid are you?"

Not as stupid as you are, mouthing off to a gang-banger with a loaded gun and a hair trigger, Lt. Rodriquez whispered. I twitched in surprise, and the dealer jumped because I jumped. He almost shot me by accident.

I ignored the voice in my head and concentrated on the threat in front of me. An epically lousy day was getting worse by the second. It pissed me off even more. "Just pick up your knife and go somewhere else, punk. Anywhere but here."

He looked at me over the sights of his .38. "No. We like this spot.

It's out of the way, no cops come through here, but it's right close to that fucking middle school. Lots of business, quiet-like," he told me. "We stayin', you goin'."

I gritted my teeth. "Not. On. My. Street."

He lost his cool. "Bitch, I'm gonna..." he yelled, stepping closer to me and waving the gun in his right hand. Like an idiot.

I stepped in, too, closing the distance more than he wanted to. A general combat rule: if you have a gun and your enemy doesn't have one, stay out of arm's reach. He lost his cool and then lost his advantage.

I grabbed the gun with both hands and slid past his right hand, twisting clockwise with his wrist and locking out his elbow. A quick yank, and the gun was mine. I let the punk out of the armbar and pointed his own gun at him.

"See, you need to keep correct spacing. Otherwise, your opponent can take your weapon away from you. Nothing worse than getting killed by your own weapon," I told him.

"You son of a bitch, give me that back, man. I'm gonna kill you," the angry dealer yelled. I decided not to point out that his threat to kill me weakened his case to get his gun back. Instead, I compromised. I popped open the cylinder and shook out the six rounds of ammunition, closed the cylinder, and gave him back the empty gun.

He wasn't grateful. He tried to club me with the steel weapon. I slipped past the haymaker and kicked his right leg- hard. My tactical boot slammed into the side of his shin, and there was an ugly snapping sound.

The guy hit the ground fast, screaming in pain and anger. I loomed over him. "I gave you a choice. You chose poorly," I informed him, borrowing a line from an Indiana Jones movie.

He responded by hurling the Smith at me. I batted it away with my left hand, swearing. "You better stop before I get really angry and something bad happens," I snapped.

The drug dealer spit on me.

"Fuck you," he said and tried to kick me in the groin with his good leg. I blocked the kick with my shin and then stepped down on his ankle, using the same leg. I raised my other foot high and smashed down on his pinned leg, halfway up his femur. There were another snapping sound and another scream.

"Are we done yet?" I growled. "I've got more. No? You want more?" I raised my foot. He held up his hands, his dark face twisted with pain.

"You broke my fucking legs, man," he cried.

"You're lucky I didn't kill you," I said. "Now get out of here."

"How, man, I can't fucking walk. And I can't drive. I need a hospital, man," he said.

He was right. I picked him up and put him in the truck. I tossed his empty gun and his knife into the truck bed and slid behind the wheel. "If I take you to the hospital, what are you going to tell them?"

"I fell down, man. I just fuckin' fell," he said, biting his lip.

"Okay. And you're done selling on my block. Make sure your people, or your crew, or whatever you call yourselves, know that. This was just a friendly intervention. After this, it gets serious, you feel me?" I asked.

"That ain't up to me, dude. But my crew ain't gonna like this," he responded, his face turned away.

We rode in silence after that. The Chesapeake General Hospital was only a few minutes away, anyway, and neither of us felt like talking.

I pulled into the Emergency drive up. There was no one outside. I put the truck into park, got out, went over to the passenger side, and picked up my passenger. Without a word, I carried him to a bench next to the automatic doors and set him down.

"Hey, man, what about my truck? I gotta answer for that, man. And the stash," he added.

I had planned on leaving the truck in the parking ramp, but hearing that he had drugs in it changed my mind. Besides, I needed wheels, I told myself. I smiled down at him. "I'll hold on to it for you. You won't be needing it for a while, anyway."

"Hey, you can't take my truck, man. That's stealing," he exclaimed.

I shook my head. "We Marines call it 'tactically acquiring,'" I told him. "I need to use it for a while. Any problem with that?" I asked, shifting my shirt a little so that he could see the butt of my Para sticking out of my holster.

He shook his head, too. "Not me, man. We cool."

I got back in the truck and put it in gear. I nodded to him and let off the brake. He flipped me off and yelled after me, "This ain't over, man. Not by a long shot."

I believed him.

CHAPTER 9

I STILL NEEDED to blow off steam, so I went for a run. Ordinarily, I hate running just for the sake of running. I run because I have to. Conditioning is paramount for a kick-ass Marine. Now I was going to use it to take the edge off.

Putting that drug dealer in the hospital was over the edge, and I knew it. I couldn't fix America's drug problems on my own or even really put a dent in them here in my hometown. I should have just kept my head down and gone on my way. But he'd pissed me off.

I didn't even have running clothes or shoes yet, but I didn't care. We'd run in our combat boots all through Basic and while deployed. So I pounded concrete in what I had; tactical pants, boots, and a blue Marine Corps sweatshirt. It's not like anyone would notice or care what I was wearing on a midnight run.

My neighborhood was mostly residential and quiet. I ran past a middle school, turned north, and saw a park. The chance to run on grass appealed to me, so I headed that way, noticing as I did that the entrance was a prime location for an ambush. There was a big arch to pass through, with an overgrown hedge on either side. There was a street light at the entrance, but it was burnt out or broken, in the oncoming gloom of night, it made the opening to the park dark as well.

My instincts told me to avoid the park, but I ignored them and ran through the arch anyway. I was angry, and angry people do stupid things. I charged through the entrance, daring anything to be there.

There wasn't. The park opened up in front of me, and I maintained my sprint, heading left. I circled the entire park at a dead run, pushing myself. By the time I got back to the entrance, I was blowing hard and settled back into an easy jog. On my second loop, the hairs on the back of my neck prickled.

I was being watched. I could feel it. My shoulders tightened, and I hunched up as I ran. I looked around as I ran, peering into the shadows and around the trees. I couldn't see anyone, but I *knew* they were there.

It occurred to me that not only had I been stupid to run into a potential ambush site, but since I'd been angry and on edge, I ran out of the house without any weapons. Not that I had any good weapons to carry easily while running. I vowed to change that as soon as I got out of this particular screw up.

I finished my second loop, still feeling eyes on me, and looked ahead at the park entrance. There was nothing there that I could see. I slowed for a moment and then put on a burst of speed and ran out of the park like the devil himself was chasing me.

Back at my house, I took a shower and ate, still feeling angry and now also foolish. I was unprepared and jumping at shadows. I needed to get it together.

One of the biggest keys to a successful mission was good intel. I needed intel badly. Thus far, all I knew was that zombies were real, and they were here, in Chesapeake. And that they were after me. I needed more than that.

I pulled out my laptop and fired it up. I wasn't a big fan of technology, but it had its place. I checked my email, trying to figure out just what exactly I was looking for online. I absently skimmed my random messages, noting that there was one from Jeremy Stevens' kid sister, Mandy, and signed out. I'd read it later.

Searching with Google, I found next to nothing on Afghani temples dedicated to the undead. Searching for red eyes brought up a movie on Netflix with Cillian Murphy and several ads for Visine.

I swore and sat back. I was getting nowhere. The internet was failing me. Maybe I needed to check "real-time" resources, that is, other Marines and armed services members. There was a bar that catered to vets and active-duty grunts that I knew. It was still relatively early.

It took twenty minutes to get across town and park in the lot at WO1. Most people didn't understand the name of the place and called it *Wo's*, which identified them as civilian pukes. Marines knew that the term meant "Warrant Officer 1," which was the owner's rank in the Corps when he got out.

The place wasn't busy; there was just a handful of guys around the bar when I walked in. A former sniper brushed past me as I went through the door and glared. I brushed it off; we had a history, and he was a dick.

I nodded at the bartender and sat down. "What'll ya have?," he greeted me, leaning against the polished wood.

"Coke," I told him. He frowned. I stared at him. Eventually, he shrugged and got my order. He set it down on a napkin in front of me and asked if I wanted to see a kids' menu as well.

"Funny," I told him, rubbing at my eyebrow with a middle finger. I threw a five down on the bar and turned away before we exchanged more pleasantries.

There were two guys on my right drinking whiskey with beer chasers. They had been overseas; they had the look. I nodded at them. They both stared at me and then nodded back.

"I need help," I announced. There was no easy way to start this conversation, and I had shitty small talk skills. "Do either of you know much about Afghani religious stuff? Not Islam, I mean older stuff."

The taller of the two raised an eyebrow. "Who wants to know? You got a homework assignment for school?" The other chuckled.

"Yeah, big comedy. Asshole. Help me out," I growled. There was no reason to bust my chops. They knew I'd been over there the same way that I knew they had been. "I got a problem."

They both nodded, like what I'd said was obvious. This conversation wasn't going very well. "Next round is on me," I told the bartender.

The two vets nodded and sat back. "What do you wanna know? You were there. They got all kinds of weird-ass cults and shit. Never tried to keep up with all of it. Just wanted to do my bit and get home safe," the taller told me, swirling his new drink around and staring into it. The other man nodded.

I sat closer. "We hit an insurgent nest—old temple. A priest or someone was running guns and underground training. He had a weird name... man...something," I told them.

The smaller guy spoke for the first time. "Not Manziel. Manzazu. Heard it, too. Not a priest, exactly."

"So what, then?" I asked.

"I guess it was more like a witch doctor. Had a big following—he controlled the whole valley. Most locals wouldn't talk about him, you know? Not that they talked to us much, anyway," the guy said, taking a pull on his beer.

"Why do you want to know anyway?" The first asked.

I shrugged. "Just curious. Former CO has some concerns about it," I said. It wasn't a lie; it was just a misrepresentation. If I was correct, Colonel LeMasters had big concerns about manzazu—he just didn't know it.

"Huh," the first guy grunted. "Over here? Odd," he said.

I shrugged again. It was one of my best moves, so I used it often. "Anything else?"

The smaller guy shifted in his chair. "Yeah, now that you mention it. Villagers were always afraid the manzazu would take their children. Not kids so much, but babies. They were paranoid as shit about it."

The tall guy set down his glass. "You're right. I remember once, we were out on patrol, found this mass grave, right? Nothing new there, huh? But this one, no adults. Just a fuckin' heap of babies. None of 'em new, ya know? They were all dried out, like mummies," he said.

I frowned. "So what did he do with the babies? They weren't like eaten or anything, just left to die of exposure?"

Both men shrugged, copying my go-to move. "No idea. We just found it, passed the info on. You know how it is," the tall one said. I nodded.

One of the other people at the bar was looking my way. He put his glass down and stood up. "Hey, you. What the hell are you doin' here? This here bar is for veterans. Not cowards," he called.

I sat still. The guy swaggered over. "I know you, asshole. You're the guy that got his whole team killed. Aren't you?" He asked, thrusting his face way too close to mine. I stood.

"Yeah, that's him," the guy said, looking around the bar at the other patrons. "This is the guy that got his mates killed and then told everyone that fucking zombies did it. Cowards aren't allowed in this bar, buddy. You need to beat it," he sneered. "This is a bar for real men."

My hands clenched at my sides. I didn't want to fight a fellow Marine. My problems weren't with the Corps. And besides, he was right. I had let my unit down. It was my fault they were dead, and I wasn't.

That's not true, Stevens argued. *It wasn't your fault,* he told me. I shook my head.

"It was my fault," I answered out loud. "It was," I repeated. I was talking to Stevens, but the guy took it as encouragement.

"Damn straight, it was your fault," he said, poking me in the chest with his finger. "You killed your men. You're a fucking disgrace. Now get out, before we throw your ass out," he growled, his alcohol-laden breath overpowering.

"I'm going," I said quietly. I tried to slip past him, but he stepped into my path. I moved the other way, and he moved again. I sighed. "I don't want trouble," I told him.

"Of course you don't. Because you're a fucking coward. How the hell did you ever get into the Marine Corps, anyway? Fucking pussy," he yelled and swung for me.

The roundhouse right was thrown from way too close and at way too wide of an angle. I reacted instinctively and blocked it with my left forearm while driving my right elbow into his nose. There was a solid crunching noise, and he went down.

One of the two guys that I'd been talking to jumped on my back, and it was game on. The rest of the bar came charging in. It didn't seem to matter that I hadn't started it.

There are little tactics or higher strategies involved in bar fights, especially one-against-the-house type fights. Things happen very quickly, with no rhyme or reason. The key to surviving is to keep moving.

I spun in a circle, throwing the guy on my back over the bar and into the bartender. As the rest of the people got into range, I grabbed two heads and bashed them together, dropping two more to the floor. Then I got tackled by at least four guys, all of us crashing into a table and then onto the floor.

Ground fighting was rough in any circumstances; fighting four men at once was impossible. I drove a knee into one and managed to punch one more but was on the receiving end of much more than I was giving.

In short order, I was pinned to the floor with a guy on each limb. Two more stood over me, kicking my ribs for all they were worth. At least one guy was on his knees, punching me in the head. Just before the lights went out, I saw the bartender push one of the guys back with the end of a baseball bat.

I woke up in the alley. My ribs were killing me, and my jaw felt dislocated. My face was covered in a sticky substance that I assumed was my own blood. All things considered, I'd had better days.

Staggering to my feet, I reached down and felt for my gun. It wasn't in its holster. I dug around in the piles of trash that I'd been dumped in and found nothing. That meant that it had to be in the bar, probably lifted by one of the helpful souls that had beaten me unconscious and relocated me.

Wiping my face with my sleeve, I limped my way to the front of the bar. I straightened up, fussed with my shirt sleeves a little, squared up my belt buckle, and walked back in.

Everyone turned my way, and conversations stopped. One of the men was getting his broken nose reset, but they stopped as well. No one moved.

I stood in the doorway; my feet spread shoulder-width, my hands relaxed at my sides. I didn't speak.

For a full minute, the entire bar was frozen in time, with no one even blinking. Then the bartender shifted. He handed a clean towel to the guy tending to the broken nose, looked at me, and asked, "Help you?"

It was so incongruous that I almost laughed. My mouth twitched, and I fought down the smile. Instead, I nodded.

"Need my firearm. Not leaving without it," I croaked.

"Can you describe it?" He asked me. One of the guys snickered. I kept my gaze on the bartender.

"Para Black Ops Recon. Double stack 1911, chambered in .45 ACP, black, Trijicon night sights, four and a quarter-inch barrel, dry weight of 41 ounces. Fourteen rounds of jacketed hollow points," I recited. My voice got stronger as I went. "No one leaves until I get it back."

Several patrons grinned at that. "You gonna kick our asses again?" One called.

"If need be. It's my gun. I get it, I leave. You go back to whatever you were doing before I came in. Simple," I said.

"And if you don't get it back?"

"Then I search each and every one of you. With or without your help," I told the room. "Maybe you throw me out again, maybe you don't. Either way, I put down more of you. And then I come back in again. Until I get my firearm back."

"Damn, boy, you are one gung ho son of a bitch," the bartender observed. I said nothing.

"And you gonna fight all of us until you get it back, or we kill you?" Another wanted to know.

"Would rather not," I grunted. "You're not the enemy. But the gun is mine."

Long looks were exchanged. Finally, the taller vet that I'd been talking to earlier shrugged and reached behind his back. His hand came forward, and in it was my Para. He set it on the table and looked at me.

"Wasn't gonna keep it. Just keeping it while you cooled off. No sense in anyone getting shot," he said.

I looked at him. "If I was the type to shoot a fellow vet, I would have done it before."

He stared back at me. "Sure," he allowed finally. He nodded at the gun.

I strolled to the table and picked it up. The room tensed and then relaxed as I holstered the Para and pulled my shirt over it. I turned to walk out.

"Hey, boy," the guy said to my back. I stopped but didn't turn around.

"That witch doctor you were asking about? Supposedly he resurrects the dead. Like, what you said happened to your unit. You be careful out there," the vet told me.

I walked out, stiff and sore but intact and still armed.

CHAPTER 10

THE NEXT THREE days were spent training, mostly inside my little duplex. I had a spare room set up for working out, with an old weight set and a heavy bag that the previous tenant had been kind enough to leave behind.

I was sore, but nothing was broken, so I pushed past the pain and did full sets of everything. Weapons' training was just dry fire exercises with the guns and attacks and defenses with the knives. It was intensive but tedious.

I spent the evenings online, trying to find more information about the manzazu. He had to be behind the hospital attack, and I thought I knew how he had gotten to U.S. soil.

Our interpreter and guide for the last mission had been killed. I had seen him literally torn apart by the zombie horde. And yet, according to the U.S. military, he was alive and well and given free transport to America. Colonel LeMasters himself sat beside him on the plane.

So Abdul-Rayef was an imposter. It only made sense that the imposter was the manzazu. Even a dumb grunt like me could see that. So I needed to find Abdul-Rayef. How to do that eluded me.

I sat at the table on the third night, staring at my laptop screen. It wasn't like I could just call Immigration and ask for him. When asked why I needed to know his whereabouts, I could see myself answering, "Because I think he's a necromancer. You know, the guys that bring the dead back to life and send them out to kill people?" Yeah, that'd go over well.

You need a better plan than that, Bates grated in my ear. *Work the problem, Marine,* he snarled.

Thanks, I replied—big help he was. If you guys are going to keep talking to me, you could at least be helpful, I told them. By now, I'd almost gotten used to hearing them speak to me.

Bates was right; I needed to work the problem.

The only person who had seen him since the raid was the Colonel, so it made sense that I had to go talk to him. I didn't have his phone number, but I knew he'd have an email listed on the VA website, being the head administrator.

It took only a couple of minutes to navigate the VA's official website and find an email address for the Chesapeake VA administrator. Trusting that a man like the Colonel would read his own emails, I sent him an urgent invitation to meet at a hole-in-the-wall restaurant the following night to talk.

There was a second message from Mandy Stevens, marked "Life or Death," but I had no idea what comprised life or death for a twelve-year-old, and I could only deal with one disaster at a time, so I didn't open it. I'd get to it tomorrow.

After that, I logged off and went for my evening run. I ran at the same time every night, and I'd been running the same route each time, as well.

I should have varied my route, but I hated running, and it was easier to just stick to the same routine. Besides, I'd picked up a new toy the last time I'd visited Bill, and I carried it with me now when I ran.

The first night that I'd run with the new Sig Sauer P938, I had put it in a clip holster and stuck it in my waistband. It didn't work very well. Things bounce and move around when you run, and what seems comfortable when walking or even running for a short distance becomes impossible when stretched out to five miles.

The little 9mm handgun fit snugly into one hand, though, and didn't weigh enough to bother me, so I just carried it in my left fist as I ran. I held it from the top, barrel pointing out from the bottom of my hand so that it was hidden from casual view and was easy to put into my right hand in position to fire quickly.

It was raining when I stepped outside, so I pulled my hood up over my head, tugged my left sleeve down to cover the little Sig nestled in my hand, and set off, trying to avoid the big puddles whenever possible.

I didn't mind the rain much; running sucked anyway. The rain kept most people inside, which let me relax a little and allow my mind to wander.

I ran past the school, lost in thought. As I swept toward the park, I registered someone else out and about. There was a guy in the same red Marine Corps hoodie that I was wearing, coming from the other way. So much for the rain keeping everyone inside, I thought.

Seeing another fitness buff running in the rain in the same hoodie wasn't anything unusual; we were near the base, and lots of guys had that hoodie. I watched him, though.

The guy turned and cut into the park fifty yards in front of me. He never even looked up at me. Clearly, he wasn't a threat. I relaxed and watched him head through the entrance.

As he went through the archway, shadows hit him from either side. It was a perfect ambush. Four dark figures dragged the jogger into the park, behind the hedge wall. I watched in shock, my brain struggling to register what I was seeing.

The guy shouted for help, breaking my brain-numb paralysis. I broke into a sprint, desperate to help a fellow Marine. I reached the arch and charged in.

The young man in the Marine Corps hoodie was down, and four people were on top of him, their backs to me. I grabbed the nearest one by the end of his shirt and yanked him off of the fallen Marine.

The man that I'd grabbed turned on me, growling fiercely, and I froze in shock. His eye sockets were blazing red fire. In the deepest recesses of my mind, I knew I should have expected this.

The undead guy reached for me, his mouth moving like he was trying to talk. Or bite me from too far away. Either way, it was creepy. From up close, I could see that his mouth was red, and there were bits of stuff hanging from his teeth.

I shoved him in the chest, gaining some precious space, and then used the space to bring the Sig Sauer up and put a round in the zombie's skull. The red glow disappeared, and the body, inert once again, fell to the ground.

By this time, though, the other three dark figures on top of the Marine had all climbed back to their feet and come after me. I stepped back to avoid getting tangled in the corpse at my feet.

It took the three an extra second to get around their fallen comrade, and in that time, I put a bullet in the forehead of the leading zombie. That one dropped, too. Two down and two to go.

I pivoted slightly to put a round in the zombie to my right, but I wasn't fast enough. Once upon a time, the thing was probably a pretty attractive female. Now, she yanked my gun arm. I lost both my sight picture and my balance, stumbling right into the thing's loathsome embrace.

Fetid breath washed over me as the undead creature buried its head against my neck. I could feel the fingers digging into my back like they were claws. Part of my soul screamed in outrage and revulsion.

I grabbed its hair in my left hand and forced its head back, away from my throat. It snapped its teeth, trying to get at me. When it opened its mouth to try again, I jammed the Sig as far in as I could and pulled the trigger.

The fingers loosened their grip on my back, and the creature slid away, its face going blank as the red glow faded from its eye sockets. I resisted the urge to kick at it in disgust.

One attacker remained, and it had worked its way around the

other corpses and grabbed me by the throat before I could shoot it. Its cold fingers were strong as hell, clamping my windpipe shut and threatening to crush my larynx.

Hunching my shoulders, I reached over the top of its arms with my left arm and trapped its hands. Then I brought the Sig in my right hand up the middle, right between its hands and in front of its face. I shot it twice and felt its grip weaken and then slide off of me.

I stepped back yet again, away from the mess, and shuddered. I'd been touched by death itself. It wasn't a feeling that I ever wanted to experience again.

Looking around, I didn't see anyone or anything else lurking, so I clicked the safety to on and switched the Sig to my left hand again. I crouched beside the fallen Marine. He was dead. It looked like his throat had been ripped out by blunt instruments; in this case, undead human teeth.

I realized that it was probably my fault that he was dead. He was wearing what I wore every night to run in, running into the same park at the same time that I went. The ambush was set for me, and he'd sprung it by mistake.

"I'm so sorry, buddy," I told him. I reached down to check his dog tags so I'd at least know who had given his life for my worthless one. My fingers had just pulled his chain out of his hoodie when he moved.

I jumped in surprise but then started checking him over in excitement. "Hey, are you there, buddy? C'mon, give me a sign. Open your eyes, pal," I implored.

The body on the ground opened its eyes. Sometimes you get what you wish for but regret it. The Marine's eyes glared balefully at me, red as the fires of hell.

"Shit!" I yelled and stumbled backward, falling on my ass. We raced to our feet—the newly undead Marine and me. I won and hastily put two rounds into the struggling zombie.

The former Marine fell back to the ground, and I looked around the park again. The same creepy feeling of being observed had returned, and it was overpowering. I *knew* something was out there. I just couldn't see it.

After a time, I gave up. Whatever I was sensing, it wasn't coming in to attack me. I looked around the scene of the ambush. The Marine was obviously twice dead; the ragged holes in his throat showed the torn and mangled carotid artery and jugular vein, and the two bullet holes in his skull had exit wounds big enough to take half of the back of his head off.

The four dark-clad bodies that had killed him had obviously died earlier. They were in various stages of decomposition, but the decomp was clear.

There was no good way to explain this. At all. Calling 911 now and sticking around to talk to the authorities would lead in one direction, and one direction only—me locked up. Either in jail or a psych ward.

There was only one thing to do, and I did it. I ran out of the park with my hood pulled tight on my head and double-timed it all the way home.

CHAPTER 11

THE NEXT MORNING, I had the local news on from the moment my eyes opened. I kept an eye on the TV during my entire workout and during breakfast. There was a developing news story: The body of a twenty-one-year-old Marine had been discovered in a park in southern Chesapeake. He was thought to be the victim of a random dog attack or possibly a feral dog pack.

There was no mention of him being shot in the head twice. There was no mention of the other four bodies that were in the park with him, all previously dead but with fresh 9mm bullet holes in their heads.

I was at a complete loss. No medical examiner worth his degree would believe that the teeth marks in the Marine's throat were from canines. Or miss the fact that he'd been shot twice in the head after getting his throat ripped out.

All I knew was that things weren't right.

Wow, you're some kinda genius, Bates mocked. "Things ain't right," he echoed. *You shoulda been an officer.*

Screw you, Sergeant. If you're so brilliant, why don't you tell me what's going on?, I challenged. There was no reply. The voices in my head weren't any smarter than I was. Which made sense if they were just imaginary.

If you had a problem and couldn't work it out in the Corps, you took it up the chain. Me being a Corporal, I would go to my Sergeant, which was useless in this case. Lt. Rodriquez was also just a voice in my head. I had no idea where our unit's Captain was, but our commander, Colonel LeMasters, was around and looking out for me. I had a meeting with him tonight.

My plan was to dump all of this in his lap. That's what officers were for. Surely he'd know what to do or come up with a plan.

I met him at his recommended restaurant precisely eight o'clock. We had a table in the back, cocked at an angle so that we both could see the front and rear exits, which I appreciated. We ordered food and then got down to business.

"You asked for this meet, Brooks. What's on your mind?" The Colonel started.

I decided not to beat around the bush. "The same guy who took out my squad is here, Colonel. You remember the attack at the hospital, right?" I asked, knowing full well that he did.

"Well, it happened again," I told him.

He raised an eyebrow. "What do you mean?"

"You heard about the dead Marine this morning, right?"

He nodded. "I did."

"I was there," I said. "It wasn't no wild dog, or pack of dogs. He got ambushed by four undead. They killed him before I could stop it. I put them down, and tried to help him."

The Colonel knew that I had more. "And?"

I held up a hand. I looked around the restaurant. I couldn't see anything amiss, but something was off. The Colonel looked at me questioningly.

"I feel like someone's watching us," I told him.

He glanced around and then shook his head. "Your imagination, son. We're fine. Go on; you were telling me about the Marine at the park."

"He was dead. I pulled his tags, to get his name, and his eyes opened. They were red, Colonel. Glowing red. He tried to kill me. I put two into him and then left," I told him, still not convinced that we were alone. I shrugged it off.

"Today, all I hear is that he was killed by dogs. No mention of the other four, or the bullets in his skull. Something's going on," I finished.

LeMasters sat quietly, digesting what I'd told him.

"I'm not crazy, sir," I said.

"I never said that you were," he replied. He wasn't looking me in the eyes, though. That was a bad sign.

"The manzazu is here, Colonel. He's after us. He set me up in the park," I insisted. "What I don't understand is why there's some kind of cover-up going on."

"Brooks," the Colonel started, shaking his head. "You do realize how this sounds, right? There's a priest that died overseas, here in Chesapeake, raising the dead and sending them after you, and then someone is covering it up afterwards. Does that sound rational to you, son?" he asked me, finally looking me in the face.

"I didn't say it was rational, sir. I said it was true," I said quietly. I stared at him long and hard. He broke eye contact first.

The Colonel looked around to make certain we were alone. He hunched his shoulders and shifted forward in his chair. "Sticking to your guns, eh, Brooks? I can't say I'm surprised. You've always been gung ho. Well, let me give you some advice: trust your instincts. Anyone that was Force Recon knows that, but I want you to keep it in mind. You're in some weird shit.

"I'm not saying that you're right, Brooks," he continued. "There has to be some explanation other than the supernatural and then a cover-up. But there have been peculiarities, no doubt. I talked with our morgue doc, and he says there was no way those two men were only unconscious and woke up. They were dead. And the condition of those bodies afterwards matches your description of what happened perfectly."

I sat forward. "Then what the hell, Colonel? Let's go find that 'interpreter' and let's get to the bottom of this."

"We looked for him, Brooks. He's in the wind. The family that volunteered to foster him while he got acclimated to America says he never met them at the airport."

"Shit!" I exclaimed, loudly enough to have our waitress look over. The Colonel waved her off and held up a hand to keep me quiet.

"So, I tried to check on your story, Brooks. I couldn't find the interpreter. The bodies from the incident at the VA were removed by government officials later that night. As for your story about last night; there's no evidence of anything that you're claiming.

"So...what do you want me to do, son?" he asked. "Officially, we've got nothing."

I shook my head in anger, biting my tongue. When I trusted myself to speak, I stared down at my plate. "Nothing, sir. That's what I expect, I guess. You're a pencil pusher now. You said it yourself. I should have known better," I said bitterly. "Thanks for meeting with me, sir," I added, rising from my seat.

"Sit down, Corporal!" LeMasters snapped, in his best field commander voice. I sat.

"Look, Brooks, I said 'officially, we've got nothing.' Unofficially, I believe enough of your story to give you some leeway. You keep at it on your end, and I'll use my contacts, both military and government, to find out more," he promised. "In the meantime, it appears that you're at risk. Watch your six, young man."

"Sir. You're at risk, too. They came to your office first, remember? He's after both of us," I reminded him.

The Colonel smiled grimly. "I'm covered. I have armed guards at my home, and there's now one at the door to my office. You just watch yourself. Take precautions; I know how headstrong you are."

We stood. It wasn't the time or place for it, but I saluted him anyway. Old habits die hard, and in my mind, I still had a mission and a commanding officer. He returned the salute and tossed money down on the table, covering our meal.

"Thank you, sir," I told him, meaning for the meal and believing in me. He nodded, the look on his face telling me that he understood.

I pivoted and started for the door, noting for the first time that two obvious military-types were sitting at a small table near the door, and watching me closely.

I spun back toward the Colonel. "They with you?" I asked, hooking my thumb at the two bruisers.

The Colonel nodded. I nodded back at him. "So you've been taking this seriously all along, haven't you? Reassigned commanders running a hospital don't warrant personal protection detail, sir," I said.

"Let's just say that there were rumors of things in Afghanistan, regarding that temple, and the man in charge, that were unsavory even by wartime standards. Some of those rumors have followed us home, it seems," he said. "I have beefed up security around me and my family."

"Good call, sir," I told him. "You could have told me when I asked. You knew we were being watched," I said reprovingly.

"Are you taking your Colonel to task, young man?" He asked, eyebrow raised.

"Sir, yes, sir," I said.

He chuckled. "Always gung ho. Fair enough, Brooks. Good night," he said and walked out, followed by his two bodyguards.

I frowned after them. The prudent thing would have been to have one guy go out first, and the second bring up the rear. Whoever the Colonel had recruited to stand watch wasn't taking their job very seriously.

I debated catching up to them and correcting their procedures or just letting them go. I decided to let them go, it wasn't my job. The Colonel was a combat vet; he could take care of himself.

My truck was parked three blocks away. It was an easy walk, but as I left the lighted area in front of the burger joint I was struck again by the feeling that I was being watched. The Colonel and his guys were gone, so it wasn't them.

I picked up my pace, moving quickly, but no longer heading straight to my truck. I crossed the street in the middle of the block, looking around to see if anyone revealed themselves. I couldn't see anything out of the ordinary, but the feeling intensified.

Scowling, I ducked into an alley and waited. No one walked by for at least five minutes. I decided that I was probably imaging things and moved away from the wall that I'd been leaning against.

Four figures came around the corner into the alley, moving fast. They were wearing dark clothing with hoods covering their heads. Their eyes burned with red fire.

I backpedaled, trying to put some distance between myself and the four of them. I looked over my shoulder to the other end of the alley, and saw four more coming at me from behind.

I turned partway and leaned against a dumpster, my heart racing. I took several deep breaths, preparing for action. My right hand found the Para and drew it out.

I took a quick step out and raised my gun. My hands met at just above chest level and the Para slid into place with smooth, practiced ease. I thumbed the safety off and sent off the first round as soon as there was a head framed in the glowing dots. I aimed right between its creepy red eyes.

The creature's head exploded in a fine mist to the accompaniment of the .45's loud boom, magnified by the narrow confines of the alley. Before the rest could scatter, I shot all three; two in the head and one center mass. The two stayed down.

The one that I'd hit in the chest staggered, recovered, and charged. I cursed. "In the head and they stay dead," I muttered. Any zombie hunter knows that. I growled and reacquired my target.

Just as it jumped for me I put two rounds into its face and side-stepped. The unthinking zombie stumbled past me and fell. I had a mental flash of myself as a bullfighter, sidestepping out from behind the cape as the bull charged straight on through.

The vision disappeared as something strong and nasty grabbed me from behind. In a reflex action not paired with deep thought, I slammed my head back into whatever was holding me. A nose crunched, and the thing holding me growled. Its arms loosened just the slightest, and I took full advantage. I slipped my hips out from against its torso and used my left hand against the back of the elbow to pop out from the undead chokehold.

I started to shoot the zombie, but had to reset my aim when I realized that I was pointing at the middle of its back. Jesus! This guy, back when he was alive, had to have been the best bouncer in town. Or the entire offensive line on a really big football team. He was bigger than my old barracks had been.

No matter. A quick raising of the barrel, a squeeze of the trigger, and the gargantuan undead was down. Followed in short order by two more of them, coming uncomfortably close to reaching my throat before I returned them to the inert matter that they'd been.

I took a big rasping breath of air, and lowered my gun. I was standing in a pile of dead bodies. Before long, someone living was going to stick his or her head into the alley to see what all the gunfire and commotion was, and I needed to be gone before it happened.

Holstering my firearm, I stepped over the last of the seven zombies that I'd just put down and walked past the dumpster that I'd leaned against earlier. Something about seven zombies bothered me.

I realized what the problem was as soon as the eighth undead creature reached out from the end of the dumpster and wrapped its arms around my neck and pulled itself up to tear out my throat.

The monster tried over and over to bite me. I spent my time alternately thanking God for the leather coat with the high collar I was wearing and trying to get the thing off of my back. The prayer worked; teeth gnashed on the leather but not on my all-too vulnerable skin. Trying to dislodge my unwelcome piggy-backer didn't work nearly as well.

We crashed into the dumpster, and then hit the side of a brick wall. Over and over I slammed the creature into it, to no avail. The sucker was holding me tight.

Looking around, I saw a ladder to back stairs hanging down. It was just over my head. I ran over to it and jumped, ducking my head at the same time. I heard a welcome thump, and felt the weight leave my back.

Freed of my burden, I took two more steps and wheeled around, gun at the level. The last of the zombie creatures was hanging from the lowest bar, its chin caught, and arms flailing. It couldn't stay there long, though. There wasn't anything anchoring it. Just as it started to slip off the rung I shot it point blank in the forehead. It dropped to the ground in an ungainly pile and stayed still.

Nothing else moved in the alley. I clicked the safety on my 1911, returned it to its cocked and locked position in my holster, and straightened up. It was definitely time to go now.

I was back to my truck by the time I heard the sirens. I wondered what the cops would make of the mess in the alley. I wondered even more what was going to make the news.

CHAPTER 12

LEADING the news the following morning was a rash of baby abductions in the Chesapeake area. Five infants, all less than a year old, had been taken in the past week. There were no clues as to who or why, and not one ransom note.

That story bothered me a lot, but it wasn't what I was looking for. Last night I had been attacked in an alley by no fewer than eight zombies, and I had left them all dead (again) in that alley. That kind of gunfire and body count absolutely had to make the news.

It didn't. I got online and googled it. Not even any wacko fringe sites had anything about it.

I thought that perhaps it was the Colonel's influence, keeping a wrap on things, but dismissed that idea. He would have contacted me to see if I was okay. And besides that, even he didn't have that kind of juice.

Giving up on the internet, I logged out and proceeded with my morning workout. I dropped to the floor and started my calisthenics. One hundred pushups later, the last five clapping, my shoulders were twitching pleasantly. My forearms were tight enough to keep me from being able to bend my wrists. Good enough.

I rolled over and did my sit ups, twisting as I rose to work the obliques. Lots of gym rats miss that; they just want the hard abs and the look. Getting hit in the kidneys sucks more than almost anything short of a committed relationship, though, so serious guys work to protect them.

A hundred and fifty sit ups later, my arms were loose again and it was time to move on. Pull ups. Twenty-five of the nasty bastards. The first ten were never that tough; the last five make me regret ever trying to be in shape. Exercise is overrated.

Unless you're doing the kinds of things that I do. I am now a one-man army, throwing myself in harm's way to protect an ignorant and innocent world from the things that go bump in the night. I bump back. And to do that, I need every edge I can get, physical or otherwise.

With that responsibility, I never skimp on the training. Ever. Damn it. Two hours later, after heavy bag work and weapons practice, I hit the shower. Time to get on with my day.

After a carbohydrate-heavy lunch, I got dressed and headed out the door. The sun was shining and I suppose it was a beautiful day to most people. Normal people, blissfully unaware of what was out there, waiting for them.

I just saw it as an advantageous time to be out and about. The bright sunlight could be used to distract and blind, and weapons being brought to bear on me would be easier to spot due to the flash. Not to mention that most nocturnal predators would be hiding right now, rather than skulking around, trying to catch me with my guard down.

So what if I'm paranoid? I have reason. It's not like last night I was attacked in an alley by eight zombies or anything. I know that there is more going on; that wasn't a random attack for no reason. They were after me.

The first item on my schedule for the day was a damn meeting with my doctor. Weekly appointments with the shrink was part of the conditions for my release, and whether I liked it or not, I had to go sit and listen to him prattle on about whatever bullshit he was required to dish out to PTSD victims like me.

At least it was a solo thing. They had taken me out of group meetings with other vets right away.

I parked my battered old pickup in the lot and went in to the VA hospital. Hospitals always make me uneasy; they're full of sick people and smell like death. The hospital; not the people. Actually, some of the people there smell like death, too. So, I'm not a big fan of them. And I had been spending far too much time in them of late.

I took the stairs to the psych wing on the fifth floor. I was the only one using them. Apparently exercise and fitness is not a big part of hospital routine. Not a shock. At least this way I knew I wasn't being ambushed or followed.

The reception area was the same as always: boring and depressing, with just a hint of disapproval on the face of the woman at the desk. She saw me come in, frowned, shuffled papers, and then spoke into her earpiece.

"Mr. Brooks, you can go in," she nodded toward the far door, like I'd never been here before. The three other people sitting in the waiting room looked outraged, like I jumped their spot in line. I walked past them without saying anything. It wasn't my fault I didn't have to wait my turn. I didn't even want to go in at all. I would have waited. The doctor had decided that it was best if I wasn't allowed to sit and disrupt the others. I guess I have an unsettling presence. That was the phrase the doc used, anyway.

Immediately through the first door was a glassed in guard station. Common practice at a mental health facility, but it's my understanding that usually the doctor's office was on the other side of the guard station.

"Mr. Brooks," the guard greeted me. "You're early today."

I glanced at the clock on the wall behind him. I was exactly two minutes ahead of last week's arrival. The best I could give him was a shrug. He was just a pencil pusher, despite the nightstick on his belt.

"Well, you know the drill, Mr. Brooks. I gotta pat you down

before you go in. Anything metal you can put in the basket here, and any other weapons you might have on you. Let's not have a repeat of last week, okay?" He asked. "You have no need for a gun here at the hospital; this is a safe environment."

Safe environment? Jerk. There was no such thing, especially in a place full of nut jobs. This wimp had no idea what constituted dangerous and what didn't. The distaste must have shown on my face, because he got upset.

"I know you think you're the shit, Brooks, but I got news for you: I'm a Marine, too, and if it were up to me, you'd be in one of these beds, strapped down with a Thorazine drip in your arm. Anybody else would be, but not you. I don't know who you know, or who you blow, but one of these days, it'll just be you and me, and we'll see, then," he ranted, getting way too much in my face for a man in need of better mouthwash.

I didn't hit him. The restraint that I showed should have given me brownie points in the doc's little ledger. Marines aren't normally known for their restraint.

"So, anyway, big shot, empty your pockets. Now," the prick commanded.

I did. I took the Para .45 out of my in-the-waistband holster and set it in the tray after dropping the magazine and stripping the round out of the chamber. Then I followed it with my trusty Emerson CQC folding knife from my right front pocket, and the little tactical flashlight from my left pocket. My wristwatch was thrown down on top of them.

The guy glared at me, so I unstrapped the Ka-Bar from my belt and added it to the pile. He still wasn't satisfied. I sighed and held up my arms to show that they were empty.

"Take out the damn gun from under your left arm, smart ass." Good catch. Maybe he really was a Marine. I took the Glock 19 from my tactical shirt and handed it to him. He took it from me and set it down without clearing it. Amateur.

"Anything else, Brooks? I can't believe they let you walk around free, carrying this arsenal. All right, let's go see the doc," he said, opening the gate and waving me to go through in front of him.

An alarm sounded as soon as I stepped through. Damn! When did *that* get put in? Leave it to the government: no money for taking care of the vets, but plenty of money to add metal detectors to the hospitals.

The security puke grabbed my arm and dragged me back to the desk. "What the hell, Brooks? What else you carrying? Now," he grumped, red faced.

I looked him straight in the eye. Not my fault you missed weapons on me, I thought. I know what you're carrying, and where. Without moving, I flicked my eyes downward, toward my feet. He crouched down and checked my left ankle. And swore.

I don't know what his problem was. The Sig P938 on my ankle was a fine gun for close quarters. It was shit in a serious firefight, but that's what the Para was for. Or the Glock. This one was strictly back up.

"Brooks, you're certifiable, you know that? Jesus, what the hell do you think is after you?" The guard wanted to know. I don't think he was serious. If he knew, he'd probably quit. Or at least give me a wider berth.

Just to show him that there were no hard feelings, I took the switchblade out of my right boot and handed it to him without his asking. He didn't seem as grateful as he should have been. I was now completely disarmed, and felt really vulnerable.

I passed the metal detector test this time, and was marched down to the doc's office. My chaperone knocked, announced me, and then ushered me in.

"Ah, Mr. Brooks. You are a couple of minutes late. That's very unlike you. Problems?" He asked pleasantly enough. Nice guy, my shrink. Guess it helps keep the crazies from wigging out, being all pleasant and even keeled.

"Dr. Sovers, he took longer at the security desk than normal.

Added a couple things to his personal armory," the guard snitched. "You want me to stay?"

"No, you can go. Thank you, Corporal Paxton," the doc told him. The guard glared at me once more to remind me to be nice and left, closing the door behind him. The doc turned his attention to me.

"So, Mr. Brooks, how are you doing this week?"

I love these sessions. "Fine."

"Any new prospects in the area of finding a nice job?"

Like someone would hire me. "No."

"Made any new friends?"

You won't let me talk to anyone, my eyes told him. "No."

After the last veiled threat he'd made, I had decided to answer him quietly in as few words as possible, to keep from getting in trouble. To keep my sanity, I allowed myself a mental response to each question, though. So far it was working.

His eyes flicked away for an instant, glancing at his computer monitor. "You brought three guns to our session today, Chase. Why do you feel the need to bring so many weapons just to talk with me? I'm on your side, remember?"

Calling me by my first name is not going to make us soulmates. "There are no sides, doc. You already explained that to me. I just like to be ready."

"Ready for what, Chase? Do you believe that there are people or things trying to hurt you?" He asked, slipping in the *things* part smoothly, trying to catch me again. I used to talk about what I'd seen over there honestly, but the doc had thought I was crazy. And I didn't want to be locked up; helpless against what was stalking me.

"No. It's just a dangerous world, doc." Which was still true, and wouldn't get me in trouble for saying. I hoped.

"Chase, you carry all of those weapons. How did you even get on the bus to make it to your appointment with me?" The doc wanted to know.

"Didn't take the bus. Drove my truck. Easier."

The doc leaned in, which of course made me want to hit him. I countered by shifting in my seat, moving back out of reach. He noticed and jotted something down in his notebook. I felt like I'd done something wrong, which made me want to hit him again.

He continued his assault. "Chase, I don't show a truck in my records. Did you buy a truck when you were released?"

"I didn't. I found it."

"You found a truck. Really? With the keys and everything, Chase?" Sarcasm. I didn't think that was normal procedure for dealing with combat vets with PTSD and a history of violence. He was really pushing buttons today.

"I got it from a guy. He didn't need it anymore," I said. True enough. The drug dealer from down the block was an unnecessary evil in my neighborhood, and I put him out of business. More or less permanently. He was still breathing, but had no need for a vehicle, since the use of his legs was a luxury he wouldn't be enjoying for the next four or five months.

"Okay, let's move on," Dr. Sovers said, sitting back. I leaned forward to match, so that he was just out of reach but easily stopped if he should draw a weapon on me. It could happen, a little voice in my head warned. "You prepare for what your enemy is capable of, not what you think he'll do," my instructors taught me. And anyone who didn't think Dr. Sovers was my enemy hadn't been paying attention.

The good doctor noticed my shift, and again made note of it in his book. I think he knew more about combat and spacing than Paxton at the security desk did. Odd, for a shrink. I raised my hand. He cocked an eyebrow at me.

"Yes, Chase? You have a question? You don't need to raise your hand, just ask," he told me, winking like I was now a favored student.

"You notice a lot about movement, doc. And spacing. You serve?"

Something flickered behind his eyes, and he covered it by adjusting his glasses. "Why, yes, Chase, I did. I served two tours, working with soldiers in Afghanistan. I was never really in the fighting, though; I spent most of my time in field hospitals and conferring with colleagues about combat stress symptoms and the like." He shifted in his seat. "I never interacted with the enemy; never saw any 'action,' if you will. Not like you did," he said.

I notice body language. It's a survival tool; one that I keep finely honed. It lets me know when I'm about to be attacked. It also serves me well as a lie detector. And the doc was now setting it off. Why he was lying didn't matter at all to me. I just wanted this session to be over. I had things to do.

"Okay, fine. Glad for you, doc. We done?"

"I'm surprised at you, Corporal Brooks. You know that we have more time, and need to address some other issues before our discussion is finished for the day," he said, emphasizing my old rank. Despite my resolve to be stoic in these meetings, I bristled.

"It's just Brooks, doc. I am no longer a United States Marine Corporal, and you damn well know it."

"Easy does it, Chase," he soothed. "It's all right. It was your rank when you were discharged, and I slipped and used it, since we were talking about serving. My mistake; I apologize." The bastard. He'd tried to provoke me into doing something that he could use against me.

I unclenched my fists and sat back in my chair. For the first time, I forced a smile onto my face. "It's okay," I lied. "I just haven't heard that in a while, and it caught me off guard."

"Well," Sovers said, seeming to be just the slightest upset that his ploy hadn't worked. "Let's just visit one other topic of discussion, shall we? Has anything else of interest happened to you since we last spoke? Anything at all?" He asked, trying to be casual.

Images of the alley, and the undead goons that had tried to kill me flashed through my mind. "No."

"Nothing out of the ordinary at all? I find that hard to believe, Mr. Brooks," Sovers insisted. "You don't carry yourself like a man who leads a boring life. I feel that you are perhaps not being honest with me. Lying to me is not the way back to mental health, and may cause your circumstances to be re-examined."

I blinked. Was the bastard really trying to get me to talk about the attack by threatening me? What the hell did he know about it, anyway? I balanced my options.

"Nope. Nothing out of the ordinary, doc. Been a pretty slow week," I told him. I'm not giving up info to someone trying to get me put away. No matter what else he threatens me with.

"Okay, Chase. It seems that you still aren't willing to trust me. That's okay, trust takes time to build. We have plenty of time to build on our foundation. We can talk more next week; I do have an early meeting with a friend of yours to get to."

I must have shown some level of interest, because the good doctor told me who he was meeting with. "I have a meeting in a few minutes with Colonel LeMasters. You remember him, I trust? He is the one that arranged for you to be seen here, rather than being kept here longer as an in-patient."

The doc stood, indicating that our session was, indeed, over. Thank God. But then he kept talking. "You should be grateful to him, you know. He is the only reason why you aren't behind bars. Or a guest here, in one of our patient wings. It is his intervention and continued interest in your well-being that keeps you more or less at liberty to roam around free and frankly, too-heavily armed. He insisted that we keep your indiscretion last week with the firearm to ourselves, and no doubt this week's as well.

"Perhaps you can thank him on your way out, Chase."

"Yeah. Whatever, doc. Later," I told him, and yanked open the door, eager to be on my way. And walked right into Colonel LeMasters, who'd been about to knock.

The Colonel was still in pretty good shape, for an old retired guy. I hit him pretty hard in my attempt to escape the shrink's office, and he barely moved. To my credit, neither did I. We kind of ended up in this awkward, half-hug, half-grappling pose in the doorway. If there'd been music, people would have thought we were dancing.

Colonel LeMasters laughed and stepped back. "Gung ho as

always, I see, Brooks. Running off to work, or just getting away from Dr. Sovers?"

I fought back the urge to salute, and settled for staring at the floor and mumbling, "Just have things to do." I'm good with words like that.

"Mr. Brooks is in a hurry to tell you something, Colonel LeMasters," the shrink called from behind me. The prick. I didn't think psychiatrists were supposed to lie. Don't they have ethics?

LeMasters looked at me expectantly. I felt like I was back in elementary school, and the teacher was waiting for me to give the correct answer. I hated elementary school. From behind me, I feel the doc put his hand on my shoulder. I resisted the almost overpowering urge to flip him over my back and break his arm. Just barely.

"Colonel LeMasters, sir. Thank you for your assistance in getting me assigned here for counseling, sir. It means a lot," I managed to get out. I really did owe the Colonel, and there was no shame in acknowledging it. It sucked having to recite it in front of Sovers, though.

I felt his fingers tighten on my shoulder. "We were just discussing Mr. Brooks' need for walking around in public being somewhat overprotected, Colonel. Perhaps you could convince our young Marine here that he doesn't need to carry the entire armory around with him. It makes me nervous, and somewhat disinclined to allow him full liberty," the doc said.

Now I really felt as like I was back in school. Like one teacher was ratting me out to another. I shuffled my feet, twisting out from under the doc's hand, and stared straight ahead. The Colonel smirked, I think.

"Well, I can see that you want to leave, Brooks. Don't let us stop you. Be sure to collect all of your things at the security desk. I left an item or two there myself," Colonel LeMasters told me. The idea that the Colonel also came in armed made me feel better.

I threw a look over my shoulder at Sovers as I left. It was the best that I could do. On my side or not, I didn't think Colonel LeMasters would let me get away with actually smacking the shrink on my way out.

At the security desk, I took great pains to put each and every weapon back in its place, slowly, while maintaining eye contact with Paxton the entire time. I should be above such things, but I'm not. He stood still and ground his teeth. I know because I could hear it. Who says life doesn't have its little moments?

CHAPTER 13

HAVING ESCAPED THE HOSPITAL, and my shrink, it was time for me to get on with my day. Against my nature, I smiled as I considered my next stop. The gun shop that I frequented was as close to Santa's Workshop as I was ever going to get, and the old fart that ran the place was as close to Santa as I would ever get. Well, on second thought, maybe he was more like the father that had been missing from my life for the past twenty years. He wasn't fat or jolly, but he did feel like family.

"Oh, it's you," Bill scowled when I slipped through the door. I felt my heart swell. He always greeted me with affection. It was almost embarrassing. Being the cynical hard case that I am, I just grunted in reply.

"What do you want, Brooks? I'm trying to work here."

"Just picking up my new sight. You said it was in," I told him.

Bill looked up at me from behind the counter. "You got night sights on that Recon of yours, Brooks. What do you need new sights for? You break something?"

Hard ass. He knew what I was there for. The buzzard was just busting my chops. God, I loved this place. "No, I need the red dot sight for my AR. The Para's fine."

"Humph," he grumbled, setting down the inventory sheet he'd been looking over. "Don't know why you bother dressing up that piece of shit DPMS you got. Not like it's a real rifle. Only cheap pussies own that brand. Shoulda got a real rifle, you ask me," he threw over his shoulder as he headed to the back of the shop.

"You sold me that gun," I reminded him. "Said it was the best bang for the buck on the market. It shoots just fine."

"Then why are you coming back here, putting more shit on it? If it works like you say it does, shouldn't need all this tweaking stuff. New flash suppressor, stock extender, red dot sight; Jesus. You kids, tricking everything out. Like a teenager with his first car, messing with a stereo. More money in the stereo than in the car itself," he called, still rummaging through piles of merchandise on a shelf.

"There!" The old guy crowed, finally snatching a small box from the top of a pile. "Don't know why I carry so much crap; nobody needs any of this shit. Just little boys with toys," he shook his head as he came back up front. "At least most of them have the sense to buy good stuff. Why you skimp on your AR is beyond me, kid. I know you got money; I mean, look at all the dough you're saving on car payments," he smirked, waving at my truck parked out front.

"Don't knock my truck, Bill. It's a family heirloom," I told him.

"Yeah. Looks like something your grandfather built by hand when he was a kid," Bill shot back. "Should take it out and shoot it. Put it out of its misery. Just don't shoot it with that DPMS of yours, it deserves better than that.

"Hey," he said, stopping as a thought occurred to him. It must have been important, to make him stop insulting me. I braced myself. "Speaking of shooting a rifle," he mumbled.

"Take a look at this, kid. Just came in." Bill reached behind the counter and brought up a rifle. I relaxed, realizing that he wasn't going to be giving me crap; he was going to show off his newest toy.

"See this? Wilson Combat. Recon Tactical. Gorgeous, huh?" he asked, holding it out to me. I caught my breath. All kidding aside, the rifle *was* beautiful. Bill put it in my hands and crossed his arms with a smile.

I swept it up to my shoulder, marveling in the balance. It slid into place as if it were destined to be there. My face must have shown something because Bill cackled with delight.

"Yeah, kid. Amazing, huh? Best damn rifle I've ever seen. Almost afraid to shoot it. Probably wanna run away with it; leave the wife for the rifle. Might not be a bad swap," he grinned.

I ran a hand down the rail, enjoying the feel. The handguard was coated in something like ceracote. I raised an eyebrow.

"Wilson Combat uses their own coating; they call it Armor Tuff. Nice, hard to ding, doesn't get hot when you run lots of mags in a hurry," Bill informed me.

I swept it up to my shoulder again, pivoting around in the store, shifting the position of my support hand from in tight against the magwell to down near the front sight. My hand slid down the polished surface smoothly. I whistled, and continued drooling.

Glancing at the muzzle, I frowned. "That's not a .223, Bill. Way too big. What the hell?"

"No shit, kid. It's a .458 SOCOM. Same lower as the .223, uses the same mags, too. Just different receiver and barrel. Designed to drop anyone in their tracks. Right away. No double-tap. Just...bang! And then," he grinned, his face lighting up like a kid at Christmas. "Then you find a new toy to play with, because this one's broken!" He laughed, pointing to an imaginary fallen enemy.

"I know what the .458 SOCOM is, old fart. It was developed for the military, remember? One shot stopper against suicide vest enemies. I just never got to see one up close or handle one," I breathed, turning it around in my hands reverently.

"Sweet," I murmured. "Nice, Bill. Holosun red dot?"

"Yep. Top of the line, not that cheap shit you just paid me for. Motion activated. See that?" He asked, pointing to the light mounted on the underside of the rail. "Turn it on," he instructed. I did. A bright light sprang from the end, lighting up the store even in broad daylight.

"Crimson Trace tactical light," the old man giggled. "500 lumens. Lights up your targets over a hundred yards away, even looking through the red dot. I put the pressure switch right by where your big-ass left thumb would sit with the magwell grip."

"I so need this rifle," I mumbled to myself. The DPMS Panther that I owned was decent, but the Wilson was talking to me...and I was listening. No, I didn't have that kind of money, and had no job prospects to warrant even thinking about buying this gun. Sternly, I reminded myself of these very pertinent facts.

But...you have a mission, the Wilson whispered. You need me. The fate of the free world may depend on it. You didn't cheap on the handgun, it reminded me. That much was true. While the Para Black Ops Recon wasn't hugely expensive for a handgun, it was still way more than a Glock or even the Sigs that the Secret Service used.

I sighed, reluctantly telling the Wilson to shut up. I set it down on the counter and glared at Bill. "Why the hell do you even show me these things? You know I can't afford it. Bastard," I scowled at him, trying my best to maintain eye contact and not look back down at the rifle between us.

"Oh come on, Brooks. You want that Wilson. You need it. I don't know how or why, and I'm pretty sure I don't want to know, but this is your AR. I was gonna keep it for myself, but you need this. I'll just hold it for you," Bill informed me. The old bastard's eyes were shining. "I'll get another one for me. I was thinking about the 6.5 Creedmoor, anyway. Better for long range. Why the hell would I need a close quarters combat monster like this?," he asked, more to himself than to me.

"Tell me why you run a business called 'Freeman Lock and Alarm' again, Bill? All you ever do is play with the guns and accessories you order. I have never seen you with a key or lock in your hands. Ever. Just the guns. Not that I'm complaining," I added as he looked offended.

"Well, I gotta pay the bills somehow," he said, pretty defensively, I thought. I looked around to see if his wife was nearby and listening. I didn't see her, but that didn't necessarily mean anything. For all I knew, she could have the office bugged.

It was a certainty that a security conscious guy like Bill would have cameras everywhere. Mrs. Freeman could have access to them, making her more or less omniscient. So I played along.

"Well, yeah, a man's gotta take care of his responsibilities," I said, nodding sagely. "Especially a man with people counting on him."

Bill snorted and looked at me. It may have been the light, but I think he glanced at a camera in the corner before saying, "Not a man if you don't take care of your responsibilities, kid. That's how you can tell a real man, or didn't they teach you that in the Corp?"

Memories of Sergeant Bates, the meanest man I'd ever met, yelling and screaming at me while I was floundering in the mud washed over me. "Don't you quit, Brooks, you piece of shit, your mates are counting on you. You let them down I will personally find you wherever you are in the world, and rip your fucking heart out myself. Do you hear me, boy?"

"I hear you," I breathed, both to Bill and the physically absent drill instructor. I shook my head, hoping to dislodge the guilty memories of boot camp and the subsequent deaths of the members of my unit.

"So, you got any Xtreme Defender rounds for .45 yet?" I asked, trying to change the subject. "I could use a box or two, if you got'em."

"What the hell for? What's wrong with jacketed hollow points?" Bill reminded me. "You know every couple years somebody comes up with some new ammo, supposed to be the best thing ever. What the hell you need those for?," he asked, shaking his head.

"Just easier," I told him. Not that it was any of his business. "Do you have any or not?"

He shook his head. "Nope. Not in stock for .45, just 9 mil. Still don't know why you want it, unless you're gonna shoot watermelons.

Cool videos, but let's wait and see how they do in the real world." He scratched behind his ear and looked at me.

"You got problems that need ammo like that, kid? You seem wound a little tighter than usual."

"What do you mean? There's nothing wrong with wanting Xtreme Defender rounds. They're awesome. Twice the permanent wound channel of a jacketed hollow point, and fast. I hear they make them for the .458 SOCOM, too," I teased.

Bill looked at me suspiciously. "You want me to order you some of those, then; .45 and .458?"

I picked up my new sight and waved him off. "No, I'm good. Nice AR, Bill. See ya," I said, and walked out the door. I think he said something else, or at least wanted to, but I didn't give him the chance. Favorite guy in the world or not, he didn't need dragged into the shit that I was caught up in.

And truthfully, I needed to get away from that Wilson Combat while I still had a modicum of discipline left. That rifle was the coolest thing I'd ever had in my hands in my entire life.

I walked back outside and tossed the knockoff red dot into the cab of the truck through the open window and then froze. Someone or something was watching me. Again. In broad daylight this time. My right hand swept down to my hip, and I pivoted almost before I saw the guy coming at me.

He froze and raised his hands. "Jesus, man, chill. I don't want nuthin, just looking for a little pick me up, you know what I mean?"

I held my Para low at my side and glared at the idiot. "What the hell? What are you talking about?"

The guy, who looked less scared than desperate, put his hands downs and looked around. He looked back at me and whispered, "Dude, I know you're the man. I just need a little, okay? Just a dime bag, or so, okay? I mean, I ain't got much, but I got enough for a taste, right? Enough to get by for now, okay?" He asked, rubbing his hands together and easing up closer than I wanted him to.

I pushed him back with my left hand, keeping my right low.

"What are you talking about? I don't know you, man. Go away," I told him. "Before something bad happens to your day." It never hurt to add a little bit of threat.

The scrawny guy cringed but didn't move away. "Aw, c'mon, man, don't be like that. I got money, okay? I'm hurtin', man. Don't leave me hangin'."

"I have no idea what you're talking about, jerk, and I don't care. Get out of here, now!" I rasped, using my best don't-fuck-with-me voice. It didn't work. Maybe I'm not as scary in the real world as I am in therapy sessions.

The lowlife actually got angry. "Hey, man, you don't have to be rude. Screw you, man, I'm a veteran; I deserve some respect! So just back the fuck off, and give me what I need. I know you sell, I seen your truck before," he said, pointing at my ride. "So don't give me that shit."

A light bulb went on above my head, slowly. This guy thought I was a drug dealer. Made sense, as I thought about it. I did take the truck from a low life that was dealing in my neighborhood. I could almost forgive the guy. Almost.

I slid the Para back into its holster and then grabbed him with both hands. Pressing him up against the truck, I got directly in his face. "I...do...not...sell...drugs. None. Never. Now beat it, okay."

The homeless looking guy wouldn't look me in the eye; nevertheless the message got through to him. He wilted in my hands, and looked away. Reminded me of a puppy I'd had once. I glanced down to make sure that the guy hadn't peed on me; the puppy used to.

He hadn't, thank God. If he had I would've given him...it dawned on me that I was about to lose control again, the way I had with the drug dealer. I took a deep breath and let it out.

I let go of the guy. I reached into my back pocket and he flinched, thinking perhaps that I was drawing my gun again. I held up my left hand to calm him, and brought out my wallet. I fished twenty bucks from it, and slipped it back into my pocket.

"Here, man. Take this. Get some food, though. Don't waste it on drugs or booze," I told him. He took the money and started to slink away.

"Hey," I called after him. "Maybe go to the VA; see if the guy in charge can help. Colonel James LeMasters. He's a good guy. And, hey," I added, my voice dropping. "I'm sorry, man."

I watched him walk off, feeling like a heel. If he really was a fellow vet, I owed him. He deserved better than to be roughed up and abused by someone thirty years younger and a hundred pounds heavier.

Shaking my head in self-disgust, I started up the old Ford and put it into gear. At least I could now move on to my favorite part of the day. I needed to go to the range and get the new red dot sighted in on my AR-15.

I kept forcing myself to concentrate on the DPMS that I owned, but somehow it kept morphing in my head into the Wilson Combat, and it was dancing with the homeless vet. Maybe Doc Sovers is right and I shouldn't be allowed out without supervision.

CHAPTER 14

I PULLED onto the relatively quiet street where I lived right around dusk. The trip to the firing range had gone well. I had my AR-15 sighted in, and beat the range instructor two out of three times on the pistol course. Shooting "zombie" targets made me smirk.

The idea of some of the "range warriors" that I dealt with, actually facing the zombies that were after me, kept me smiling as I grabbed my gear from the bed of the truck. Most of those wannabes would piss themselves, just seeing the things that I've seen.

The smile faded as shadows moved. The streetlight closest to my duplex was usually burnt or broken out, but it was still light enough to see shapes. And I saw at least three of them move. Trying to look natural, I shifted the bag to my left hand and crouched slightly, the better to move quickly if necessary.

A black man stepped out from behind the shrubbery in front of the doorway. He nodded at me. "Hey." Two shadows shifted closer; one from each side.

I stared back at the man, pretending not to notice the pair flanking me. The threat level was high, but I relaxed just the slightest, seeing that the guy in front of me was still alive. For the moment—it depended a lot on what he wanted from me. Carefully, I unzipped the top of the bag.

"Hey," the guy repeated. Apparently education wasn't high on his list of accomplishments. Maybe he'd missed the vocabulary portion of the curriculum. It didn't matter; his shortcomings weren't my problem. Unless he made them my problem.

"We got a problem, bro," he announced. So, it *was* going to be my problem. I sighed, and nodded back.

"What's that?"

"You got Johnnie D's ride, man. We use that truck to...distribute our product to people. They kinda recognize the truck, kinda like the ice cream man's van, you know?" He asked, keeping his voice friendly and his hands at his sides. I wasn't fooled. I'd seen him before. He was a violent drug-dealing jerk, and he wasn't alone.

"He wasn't gonna need the truck for a while. I'm borrowing it," I told him. "Didn't know I needed your permission." Sometimes I'm good with people.

"Bro, it wasn't your call. See, it's actually *my* truck, and D just uses it, right? And so now, we got us a problem," the jerk informed me. Again. Maybe he thought I was slow.

Maybe I was. "I don't see it. He was using your truck, and now I am. If you need it back, I'll drop it off after I'm done with it. You still dealing on the corner of Sixth and Lamont, right?"

He took another step closer. "You ain't too bright, are you? You stole our truck, and you put Johnnie D in the hospital. Now, you costin' us money, bro, taking our delivery truck outta the system we got in place." The guy glanced to his side, liked what he saw, and brought up his hand.

"Now, man, you gonna give me back my truck, plus all the money you got, and maybe whatever's in the bag, too," he sneered, pointing the gun at me. I made a sour face. Piece of shit Jimenez 9mm. If I had to die, it shouldn't be by getting shot by a crappy gang-banger using the cheapest handgun on the market.

I nodded in the direction he'd looked before pulling the gun.

"You really think that guy is gonna help you? You're gonna need more help than that to take me tonight, bro," I said, emphasizing the *bro* to insult him a little. Angry combatants make bad decisions.

"I got more help, wiseass," he snapped, waving to his left with the gun. It was the opening I needed. I swept the DPMS out of the bag and slapped the end of the barrel down on his wrist. He dropped the JA-Nine and swore.

By the time the curse hit the open air, I'd pushed his arm down and swept it around behind his back with my rifle, the move ending with him on his knees, arm pinned behind his back, and the muzzle of the .223 pressed up against the back of his skull.

"Step out," I called. No one moved. I wrenched upward, perhaps a little more than necessary.

"Oww, shit, man, you're breaking my arm. Alright," he complained. He raised his voice and called to his invisible assistants. "Come on, man, come in. Don't do nuthin' stupid," he said. I agreed with him. There'd been enough stupid for the day.

"Hey, we don't gotta do shit," a voice came from out of the darkness. "He don't even got a magazine in that AR, man."

I smiled. Not bad, for a drug dealing civilian. Without taking my eyes off of my captive, I said, "Two problems with that, as I see it. One, I can still break your buddy's arm in less than a second. Two, this particular AR-15 can fire without the mag as long as there's a round in the chamber. Wanna bet there's one left?"

I leaned in and told my companion that he needed better employees. "Your boys don't listen to you so good. I'd watch out for them."

Rustling sounds coincided with two more low lifes coming out into the open, one on either side of me. Both of them were armed, and both were ugly.

"Now what, asshole? You only got one shot, and there's three of us," the uglier one growled. "How you take all of us with only one shot?" He asked, coming closer and raising his gun. I glanced at his hand and swore. Another Jimenez. Figured. Chesapeake couldn't even get decent gangs.

I let the pressure off of my captive, just enough for him to climb back to his feet. It encouraged the other two to move in, thinking that they had me. When they were in range, I twisted my AR like it was a big steering wheel, flipping my captive completely over, and into the first, uglier bad guy. They went down in a heap.

While they were still falling, I pulled my AR out from under the first idiot's arm, and slammed the butt right into the last guy's larynx. He went over backward gurgling and clutching his throat with both hands.

Taking my time, I put the DPMS back into the bag, zipped it closed, set the bag on the hood of the truck, and picked up one of the JA-Nines. Checking to make sure it was loaded and the safety was off, I pointed it at the leader of the thugs.

"Now, where were we? Oh yeah, we were talking about my truck. You were telling me that the insurance on it was good at least until the end of the month, and that the tags were good, right?" I asked.

The head douchebag scowled, gingerly moving his arm in a circle. "Hey, man, you didn't have to break my arm, dude. Shit, we was just sent to talk to you. Didn't need to go all Rambo on us."

"You chose this, asshole, not me. You're lucky I didn't shoot all three of you," I told him. "I still might, or at least I'd think about it, if I wasn't so scared that this thing would jam or blow up in my face. Seriously," I grumbled, "how can you use these? They're heavy as hell, only shoot 9mm, the slide isn't even steel, it's some zinc crap, and they give you slide bite. This is not a gun that's gonna get you laid," I informed the trio.

For some reason, I was feeling eloquent tonight. So, I continued talking to my captive audience. "Yeah, you need to up your game, guys. You need a gun that can be your faithful companion, steady and reliable. Not some piece of crap that will let you down when your life depends on it," I said, feeling a small jolt of deja-vu. This was starting to sound like Bill, lecturing me on the Wilson Combat Recon Tactical that I'd seen earlier.

"Hey, fuck you," the third guy said, sounding a little garbled after getting hit in the throat. "You caught us off guard. Next time, you're history, asshole."

I frowned, disagreeing with his assessment, but there was a chorus of agreement from the other two guys on the ground. Maybe it was time for a reality check.

"Umm, this is me, standing up, holding the gun, and you assholes on the ground, without your guns. This isn't the time to talk big, in case you're wondering," I told them, trying to be helpful. "And I wouldn't do that, either!" I snapped, kicking the knife out of the leader's hand, just as it cleared his pocket.

The attempt to draw another weapon on me pissed me off. Here I was, trying to be reasonable after they'd come to rob and hurt me, possibly even kill me, and I was going easy on them. This was how they were going to reward me? Assholes.

"Seriously? You pull a knife on me, while I'm holding your own gun on you? What are you, stupid?" I asked. The guy just glared at me, holding his twice injured wrist in his other hand.

I glared back at them. "What the hell else you got in your pockets? Come on, empty them out," I commanded, aiming the blackened pistol directly between the first guy's eyes. Truth be told, that Jimenez was starting to grow on me. I kinda liked the balance and heft. I was starting to want to shoot it, and see what it was like.

Unfortunately, the thugs complied, and dumped all of their belongings on the ground, albeit grudgingly. Three massive wads of cash overlapped one another, amidst a pile of coins, knives, condoms, and cell phones. And several packets of white powder lay there as well.

"Wow," I breathed. I hadn't seen that much cash in a long time. The rewards of an evil lifestyle, I suppose. Didn't seem fair, them having all that money, and me not even being able to afford to outfit myself properly for my mission.

I swear the Wilson started whispering in my ear again, even from a distance. It told me that I could take their ill-gotten gains, and put it to good use. Specifically, it would pay for the rifle I'd dreamed about.

Shaking my head, I told the voice to go away. I was not Robin Hood. Stealing from the rich to give to myself wasn't right, even if life wasn't fair.

While I was having this argument with myself, one of the guys made a move. The really ugly one threw a knife at my face while jumping to his feet, in what he probably thought was a blazingly fast move.

I knocked the knife down with the barrel of the pistol, while stepping into his lunge and slamming my open left hand into his sternum. He went down hard and fast. The other two hadn't even moved. Maybe they were smarter than they looked. Perhaps his move was fast enough to catch them off guard. Probably not, though; it hadn't seemed like much to me.

It did piss me off even more, however. A lot. I kicked the guy in the ribs, just to make sure he got the point, and looked down at their stash again. They didn't deserve or need all of that stuff. The knives were crap, so I left them alone. I touched the wads of cash and hesitated.

"Hey, man, don't take our money. We gotta answer for that," the leader whined. I pointed the Jimenez at him and he quieted. A different voice took up with me.

Take it, the Wilson crooned. *You need it, and they don't. They owe it to you after this, and they know it. Take it, take it, take it.*

I shook my head. It's not mine to take, I told the rifle, as sternly as I could. It whispered back immediately, reminding me that I'd already taken their truck. My resistance crumbled as I realized that the imaginary voice in my head was right.

There was over $4,500 wrapped up in the three rolls of bills. Unbelievable. I peeled off just over three grand, stuck it in my pocket, and threw the rest back on the ground. I straightened up and scowled at my guests.

"This is how it's going to work," I told them. "You shitheads are going to leave. Without the truck. You can keep your phones, those piece-of-shit knives, and the condoms—the last thing this planet needs is for you to reproduce. I am charging you an asshole sufferance fee of thirty-one hundred dollars, non-refundable."

There was some muttering at that. I slapped the offender in the back of the head with my open hand and explained things to him. Some people need more help than others. "Look, it's not even all of your cash, just what I need for right now. I'm even going to give you back your guns, for all the good they'll do you.

"But," I warned, "This ends here. You clowns bother me at all, at any time, and I will simply put a bullet in your skull and bury you at sea somewhere. You got it?" I asked, using my mean voice again. It worked better this time. It usually works better when I'm heavily armed.

There were grumbling, half-hearted sounds of acceptance from the area by my feet. I stepped back, and they got up off of my lawn. Slowly. They collected their stuff, tried to regain their dignity, and started limping down the driveway.

"Hey!" I called. They turned. I walked after them. I clicked the safety on the JA-Nine I was holding, reversed it, and handed it back to the trio's leader. He took the gun, hefted it, and stared at me.

I stared back, without blinking. After a moment or two, he broke eye contact and turned away. One of the others said something to him, and he swore and gestured toward the street. They walked away, gradually disappearing into the night.

Standing in the driveway, I stayed still well after they were out of sight. If it wouldn't have gotten in the way of my mission, I would have allowed myself to mentally tally the similarities between me and Clint Eastwood.

Luckily, being a purposeful sort, I didn't let myself do that.

CHAPTER 15

WHEN I AWOKE the next morning, I immediately went to my laptop. A half formed idea had popped into my brain at some point in the night, and it was still fresh in my mind when I woke up.

I pulled up Google Maps, and typed in "Chesapeake, VA." In mere moments I had an aerial view of the area in Chesapeake where both attacks had occurred. They were widely separated, but between the two locations was a city park. That would make it easier for them to move around, but zombies roaming around an open park would hardly be subtle, I told myself, looking for more answers.

My eyes narrowed as I saw it. Off to the side, in the southeast corner of the park, was a cemetery. More to the point, it was a mausoleum. The same high water table that prevented most homes in Chesapeake from having basements also created a problem with burial sites. Many older cemeteries used aboveground vaults for final resting places.

Those vaults could provide a perfect hiding place for somebody to stash zombies. Or create them, for that matter. I had no idea how this was being done, but it had to be done somewhere, and a mausoleum was as good a place as any.

I studied the map. Google apparently had a new feature that

allowed you to zoom in on real footage of the location you were researching. Amazing. Fifteen years ago, you couldn't get this kind of intel on a target that our elite forces were trying to infiltrate, and now, any casual Tom, Dick, or Harry could pull this up on a damn smartphone.

I used the feature to its full advantage. There were no fences, no guards, no security of any kind that I could see at the cemetery, just a low wall separating the mausoleum from the rest of the area, and then the park was right across the street.

Getting to the park would be easy, then, but with everything so out in the open, it would be more of a challenge to check out the structures themselves. At least in broad daylight. I could go pay a night visit to the cemetery and avoid unwanted attention.

Not likely, I told myself. Tactical advantage be damned. There was no way in hell I was going to go check out a mausoleum at night. Not after being attacked by zombies twice. There was brave, and there was stupid. I could be one without being the other.

That declaration was greeted by a freaking chorus of derision in my head, as various voices laughed, chuckled, or accused me of being delusional. Assholes. I wasn't nearly as dumb as some of them seemed to believe.

So, I told myself, you're going to pay the cemetery a visit this afternoon, while the sun is still up, and check out the crypts. What are you going to need? I took stock. Obviously, I couldn't take my AR-15; people notice guys walking around with assault rifles.

The Para was going with me, of course. The Recon was my best friend, and unlike the voices in my head, never talked back or thought I made bad decisions. I set it on the table, along with two extra magazines.

After some deliberation, I added a short pry bar to my normal arsenal. The pry bar could get me into a crypt, and in a pinch, be used to take out a zombie or two, quiet like. It was small enough to carry under my jacket, as well. I smiled happily. Who says I can't do subtle?

I decided to go on foot, even though the cemetery was three miles from my house. It was an easy walk, and if I needed to melt away unobtrusively, it would be far easier on foot. It wasn't like I was carrying anything heavy; this was mostly a reconnaissance trip. And if the unthinkable happened, and I got overwhelmed, I was pretty sure that I could outrun dead people.

Shortly after two in the afternoon, then, I stepped carefully out of my house, checking for gang visitors, shrugged my shoulders to settle the crow bar I was carrying, and headed off toward Memorial Gardens. Once again, the sun was shining and it was a beautiful day.

Looking around, it was hard to believe that I was out and about in the sunshine, hunting for the lair of undead creatures. It was entirely too surreal. In fact, it was almost enough to make me doubt my sanity.

Come on, Marine, get your head out of your ass, I could hear Bates growl. *You're stupid as hell, but you ain't crazy.* That helped.

I was walking with my hat pulled low, shades on, and head down, when it occurred to me that I must look like the guy at the end of the block, selling drugs. I wasn't doing anything wrong; in fact, I was the good guy. I should walk like it. There was a difference between covert and furtive. I didn't want to slink.

Forcing myself to relax, I stood tall and proud, like a Marine on parade, and strutted down the sidewalk like I owned it. I even turned my hat around, so the bill was on the back, like a catcher in baseball. I'd seen some pro football players do that, and it was pretty common for our snipers, too. As long as it wasn't sideways I'd be fine.

I reached the park with only a few cursory waves or nods from people. I looked around the fairly small and very open area. There were several families scattered around, with picnic baskets and coolers. A half dozen or so college kids with Frisbees, the random jogger or two on the grass, and one couple walking what looked to be a moose with no antlers but had to be a dog of some sort, filled out my scan.

No one seemed to pay me the slightest bit of attention. It was kind of like high school. That was fine; I was used to it by now. It left me free to do my job. I walked right through the middle of the civilians, all happy and carefree in the sunshine, secure in the knowledge that they were safe from all harm.

I crossed the quiet road that separated the park from the cemetery and walked respectfully between the rows. Dead and gone or not, people deserved the dignity of not being stepped on and walked over.

Reaching the wall that divided the normal graves from the older crypts, I glanced around. It appeared that I was the only person on the cemetery side. I nodded in satisfaction. Go time.

Impatient, I hopped the wall, rather than walking to the entrance. Unconsciously, I had drifted toward the largest of the buildings, and I wanted to start there. It was the second to the last one in the back row, with trees behind it.

The granite sides were old but in perfect repair. The marble slabs at the entrance gleamed in the bright sun. I studied the door. "Shit," I grumbled. The door was stone, with interior hinges, and looked to be impregnable. It also looked like no one had used it in eons. It was well maintained and clean, a testament to the mausoleum staff, but there was no sign at all that it had been opened this century.

While shaking my head in disgust, the last crypt caught my eye. It was almost as large, and looked much older and in considerably more disrepair than the one I had been interested in. I stepped closer.

The walls on this crypt were stained and partially vine covered. A section of the roof had fallen in, and the whole cottage-sized thing smelled of rot. There was a big granite slab propped against the door, with an engraved warning to leave the dead to lie in peace on it.

My skin crawled, and I swear that the temperature dropped ten degrees when I read the inscription on the slab. I took a step back and looked around. I saw no one. Shuddering, I leaned back in to study the door itself.

Strangely, the door was wooden. Heavy, old, and stained, but wood. That was bizarre, since the other doors here were stone. It also had metal hinges on the outside. That meant that the door opened outward; also weird. Most old buildings had exterior doors that opened inward.

I shone my pocket flashlight on the hinges. They were clean and oiled, totally out of place on this decrepit old building. My pulse quickened. Clearly, I was on the right track. I just wasn't sure that I wanted to be proven right.

Setting my shoulder to the marble, I shoved, trying to pivot the slab around and out of the way of the door. It didn't work. The slab tipped over, landed with a spectacular crash, and broke in half. Shit. So much for subtle.

Working faster, I stabbed the pry bar between the door and the frame. As solid as the oak door was, it had no chance against a motivated Marine. It shrieked in protest as I wrenched it out of the frame. I cringed because of the noise and then just gave up. After dropping the marble slab, my mission was no longer covert, anyway.

The door came free with an audible sucking sound. I dropped the pry bar and swung the door open wide, letting sunlight into the crypt. It didn't penetrate the darkness much.

I blinked, trying to make out anything inside. It was murky as hell in there. I took a step closer. I sensed movement. A pair of red eyes stared back at me. And another. And another. I froze in shock. There were at least a dozen pairs of baleful glowing eyes staring unblinking, right at me.

There was a rushing sound, and I knew that they were coming to get me. I'd really stepped in it this time.

Stumbling backward, I stuck the light back in my pocket and reached for the door. If I could get it closed quickly enough, maybe I could keep the zombies from getting out. My fingers caught the edges of the oak, and I heaved, pulling my body out of the way at the same time.

At least, that's what I tried to do. In reality, my heel hit the back of that giant marble slab, and I went down, while at the same time slamming the door into my head as hard as I could. It would have been funny as hell if it wasn't likely to end up killing me.

My head rang like an oversized dinner bell for the undead, and I shook it, trying to clear it before I ended up an hors d'oeurve. I could see the leading edge of the horde reach the doorway. They paused just the slightest, probably because of the sunlight, and I took advantage.

I may be clumsy, but I'm not totally inept. I pushed into a back roll, putting some distance between me and the zombies, and came to my feet. There were four of them outside the door already, and the rest were streaming out faster than they ever seem to move in the movies.

Containment was now out of the question. Damage control was my main priority now. Actually, I realized as the first of the creatures cleared the slab and reached for me, survival was my first and most important priority. Never let it be said that I didn't have a tremendous grasp of the obvious.

I thrust out with the pry bar that was still miraculously in my right hand, driving it into the throat of my most immediate enemy. The thing gurgled and went down, unfortunately with both hands wrapped around the pry bar. My one hand, covered in whatever slime was oozing out of the undead creature, had no chance, and came off.

At least three more of the damn things were almost on top of me; I had no way to recover my primary weapon from wherever that first one ended up. I snatched my Para from its holster on my back hip and dropped the row of three in less than two seconds.

The next row was on me by then, though. Two seconds may not seem like much time at all, but in a fight, two seconds can be an eternity. In the time it took me to put a round in each forehead, the second wave was able to climb over the broken marble and crash into me.

I went down in a pile of the undead. Even while struggling to get free, my skin crawled. I was being smothered by decomposing flesh. I was pretty sure that this would result in yet another therapy session. If I survived.

Something hard clamped down on my leg and I panicked. In the movies, any bite from a zombie that draws blood leads to death and then turning into a zombie. Definitely not a future that I wanted any part of. I kicked out, hard, and shoved against the pile on top of me.

The pile shifted, and I clawed my way out, intent on blowing away whatever was still attached to my lower leg. I had just swung my gun down to eliminate the ankle biter when I heard a little girl's voice.

"Daddy, what's that? Why are those men trying to eat that other man?" A cutesy grade schooler asked from far too close. I heard a man swear, and then the girl screamed in terror.

I yanked my attention from my leg to where the girl and her father were. The stupid asshole had wandered over, apparently to see what I was up to, and brought his kid with him. And now they were under attack.

One of the zombies was grappling with the man, and another had just grabbed the girl when she screamed and I looked over. The guy wasn't in as immediate danger as the girl was. The zombie lifted her toward its mouth, while she flailed ineffectively and shrieked.

They were twenty-five yards away, and the girl was in front. I had less than a heartbeat to decide what to do. Did I take the shot, and risk hitting the kid, or wait for a better chance, and risk being too late? I took the shot; what choice did I have, really?

The zombie's head exploded, showered the wailing girl with brain matter, blood, and even less savory things. At least she was alive. Maybe we could go to therapy together. Some shrinks offered group rates. Back to my previous problem.

My next shot took the top of the zombie's head off from just above where his jaws were clamped shut on my ankle. Unlike a pit bull, the zombie's jaws unclenched and fell away once the rest of body was gone.

I lurched to my feet, smacking a zombie in the face with my gun to gain some space. The little girl's father was now in more serious trouble. A second creature had grabbed him, and he wasn't faring well with two of them at once. Idiot or not, I couldn't just let him die. His kid needed a father, and I sure as hell didn't want the job.

The closer of the two wasn't a problem; I took it down with one shot. The second one kept moving, and the guy wasn't helping me at all. He kept moving, too, putting his head in the way. I considered taking the shot anyway, just to be done with it. After all, I had my own problems. There were at least five more trying to get to me, not to mention the other five or six that had gone lumbering toward the park in search of fresh victims.

I lined up the zombie's head in my sights and tightened my grip on the trigger. The good guy's head was right behind the creature's though, and no matter how they do it in the movies, I knew that the round would go through and take out both of them. Which was unacceptable. I swore and leaned as far to the right as I could, changing my angle just enough...and dropped the second zombie.

I turned back to my oppressors, since they were trying to drag me back off of my feet. I snapped off a quick round at the closest and lined up the next, pulling the trigger before I realized that I'd missed the first one. The one at point blank range, with my sweatshirt in its rotting hands, trying to pull my neck closer to its mouth.

"Damn it," I yelled, clubbing the thing on the head with the Para. The heavy handgun did decent damage as a melee weapon, but that really wasn't what it was intended for. It failed to kill the zombie, but it did make it look even more grotesque. While I tried to keep it off of me, I twisted, using it as a shield so that the other three couldn't get their hands on me.

It was a macabre game of keep away, with me as both contestant and prize. I heard screams from the direction of the park now, as well as the continuing screams of the little girl. The game had to end, and fast.

Stepping back with my left foot, I twisted my right shoulder forward, thrusting the gun into the open mouth of my dance partner. I pushed down with my hand, which tilted the barrel end up, and pulled the trigger. The top of the zombie's head lifted completely off, which made me think absurdly of the old line about people "flipping their lid," and then I could hear Sgt. Bates bellow at me to keep my focus.

He was right, as usual. The dead thing dropped, and I'll be damned if my gun didn't get stuck in its jaws. I yanked hard, and even put my foot on its neck for leverage, but the Para refused to come out. I felt another zombie's hand land on my back and knew I had no more time.

I let go of the gun and drew the largest of the knives that I had on me. I spun, slamming the eight-inch serrated blade into the side of my attacker's head. This weapon I could and did wrench right out of my enemy's skull.

Which left me with two. Eight, if you counted the six that were ruining the picnickers' day over at the park. The two attacking me were no match for a pissed-off Marine with civilians to rescue. I had them down in less than five seconds, and then I re-sheathed the knife and pried my gun out of the dancer's jaws.

By the time I had my gun back in my hands, though, the last six had all crossed the road and were launching themselves at the people in the park, very few of whom had shown the good sense to run. I could see one of the college-looking guys trying to hit a zombie with his Frisbee.

"Good luck with that," I snorted. All that education, and that's what he came up with? Wow. At least he had help; the other guy was trying to pull the zombie away from the Frisbee-wielder.

I looked further. The couple walking their dog seemed okay, since the giant canine was between its owners and the zombie trying to get to them. My money was on the pooch.

Two zombies were harassing a jogger, who managed to trip and fall down even as I watched. It was just like in the movies, I marveled. "I'll bet you five bucks he twisted his ankle," I told the voices in my head. For once they were silent. Probably afraid to take me up on the bet.

As I sprinted toward the guy, I looked for the last two zombies. I found them closing in on a family that had been out for a picnic. One of the zombies had a paper plate with what looked to be potato salad stuck to its shoe, and the other was kicking its way through the overturned basket on the ground.

I had a fairly clear line of fire on those two. They were a long ways away, though, and I was running full out. I know in the movies, shooters are always making it look easy, scoring bulls-eyes while doing cartwheels or flying through the air, and of course, running. In truth, moving while shooting is one of the hardest skills to master.

The first day I had tried to walk toward a target, firing at the same time, it was discouraging, to say the least. I had no idea how much I bounced up and down as I walked. Several of my shots missed the silhouette altogether, and the rest weren't even close to where I'd aimed them.

So, I was less than optimistic about blazing away while running. If I missed by too much, I was going to ruin someone's day for good. I didn't have a lot of choice, though. These things had to be stopped. So far, no one had been killed or even hurt by the undead I'd unleashed, and it needed to stay that way.

I sent a silent prayer toward the God that looks over Uncle Sam's Misguided Children (that old USMC joke), and emptied the rest of my magazine at the picnic crashers. At least two of the five rounds hit their mark, and the zombies dropped.

Dropping a magazine, pulling out a fresh one, and slamming it home while running is also not nearly as easy as it looks on cop shows. I knew this because I had to practice this over and over again while in Recon.

Many times the magazine would end up on the ground, several feet behind me. I wasn't special; it happened to all of us.

It happened to me on this day, too. I had to come to a complete stop, back up, bend over, pick up the mag, and put it in. At least I had gotten close to where the jogger was trying to crawl away from the attackers.

I took careful aim as both creatures stood over their fallen prey. I don't know what they were waiting for, but I was grateful. With them standing and the guy on the ground, I at least had clear lines of fire. The way my day was going, I needed a break. It took me three shots before they fell, but for combat shooting at twenty-five yards, it was good enough. Two more down and two to go.

I heard the dog growl, so I looked that way first. The couple had shown good judgment and dropped the dog's leash. Freed, the huge mastiff had leapt on the monster threatening its masters and apparently torn its throat out. At least, I didn't see any movement out of the thing as it lay beneath the ferocious pet.

"Good dog," I said, turning to check in on the college boys with the Frisbee. Maybe by this time they'd figured out that they couldn't smash the zombie's skull in with a plastic disc. Probably not, I thought. They hadn't looked to be the best and brightest.

They had the thing on the ground, at least. It was trying to grab them, and they were taking turns kicking it. The two didn't seem to be causing any damage, but they were carrying the fight to the monster. My estimation of them went up a notch.

Taking a little more time, since they had the situation in hand, I jogged over and put a round in the back of the zombie's head. It flopped on the ground and lay still. The two college guys looked at me like I was some kind of criminal.

"Dude, what the hell? You can't just shoot somebody like that... it's murder," the one still holding the Frisbee said. The other one nodded in agreement.

"You're kidding," I wheezed, totally out of breath and patience. This wasn't exactly the hero's welcome that I'd expected. Morons. I looked over to the jogger; surely he'd be more grateful.

The man was still on the ground, dragging himself away from the two dead goons I'd shot. Apparently the ankle injury was enough to keep him from even standing.

The picnic family was huddled together, glaring at me like I'd kicked over their picnic basket and stepped in their potato salad myself. I shook my head at them and swiveled to check on the first two that I'd rescued.

The dad had his kid in his arms and was hustling toward a white minivan in the parking lot. Good plan, I thought. I should think about doing the same. Pretty soon, the cops were going to show up, and I didn't really have a good explanation for all the carnage.

I counted it as a victory that no one was hurt or showed any sign of being bitten. That thought reminded me that I had been chomped on. Bending down, I checked my ankle out carefully, afraid that my days as a living, breathing human might be ending soon.

No punctures. I sent quick thanks heavenward to whoever had invented denim. My blue jeans were slobbered on, not to mention covered in blood and brains, but they had held up. *That's the value of quality equipment*, I could hear Sgt. Bates reminding me. He sounded smug.

No words of encouragement or congratulation; just approval of my pants. Figures, I grumbled and ran back to pick up my discarded magazine. There was no way I could police my brass, but I was not about to leave a forty dollar mag behind. Not on my watch.

I took a last look around the park. Things looked under control, for the most part. I noticed that the father of the picnic party was pulling out his cell phone, whether to call the police or take pictures I couldn't tell, but either one was bad for me.

So I hoofed it. I pulled up the collar of my coat to make recognition more difficult for the cops, and ran off, parallel to where I needed to go. After five minutes of full on sprinting, I congratulated myself on making my escape and slowed to a jog.

Just as I started to congratulate myself on getting out of what could have been a huge mess, I remembered that I left the crowbar back at the scene, covered in blood, guts, brain matter, and my finger prints.

To make matters worse, I had that nagging feeling that I was being watched again, despite my evasive tactics. The feeling stayed with me the rest of the way home.

CHAPTER 16

IN WHAT WAS BECOMING an unwelcome habit, I spent my morning and daylight hours hiding in my house, waiting for the police to show up at my door. Yesterday's activities didn't take place in the dark somewhere private; I had engaged the enemy in a public park in front of witnesses.

I waited all day in vain. The police never showed. There was no knock at my door. It was driving me crazy. It got so that I wished they would show up. That was what was supposed to happen. In the real world.

I had no idea what was going on in this bizarro world. It was like this supernatural force was at work, trying to get me, and no matter how much damage and destruction I caused, no one noticed. It was enough to make me doubt my sanity.

Maybe Sovers was right. Reanimated corpses were impossible. I knew that. But since they been attacking me anyway, I accepted that they were real. What if they weren't?

I sat at my desk, questioning my sanity. Maybe I was delusional, like Doc Sovers said I was? Shit. I got up and went into the bathroom, to stare at my reflection.

The big creepy guy staring back at me didn't have a mark on him.

Nothing to show he'd mixed it up with a dozen of the undead the day before. I saw the man in the mirror shake his head at me in disappointment. I didn't blame him.

I pulled my Para from its holster and examined it. Damn my Marine Corps fastidiousness: there wasn't a speck of anything on it. It gleamed in spotless perfection, prettier than it had been the day I brought it home. I slid it back into place.

A small flashbulb went off above my head, apparently too high to show in the mirror, since I didn't see it reflected above my image. Didn't matter, I still had an idea. My pants. I hadn't done laundry yet.

I pulled them out of the hamper and wrinkled my nose. There was my damn proof. My tactical pants reeked of death and other shit. The left pant leg was stiff with goo and what looked to be a rotting tooth.

Dropping the jeans back into the hamper, I sat on the floor. My first feeling was one of relief. I wasn't crazy, and I hadn't been imagining the entire thing. My second feeling was one of disbelief. Only an idiot would be relieved to find out that he had been attacked by a dozen zombies, and that he didn't just need his medication level adjusted.

I wasn't alone in that assessment. I could hear Lt. Rodriquez and Sgt. Bates arguing over whether or not that made me better or worse. Bates said that I was worse, since I was stubborn enough to insist that I was right even if it meant people could die. Rodriquez countered with the notion that I could bring peace to the guys in my unit by figuring this out and putting the zombies out of business permanently.

I liked that idea. "Fucking A," I grunted and surged to my feet, gun back in my hand as if by magic. I pointed it at the guy in the mirror, who matched me with his own cannon. Neither of us blinked. "I am going to put an end to this shit," I told him, and simultaneously we holstered our firearms and nodded.

So everything was real. For some reason, the police and the news weren't getting to see what was going on. There was a cover-up happening, at a high level. But I knew one thing for certain.

I was being hunted. Somewhere out in the dark, this fucking manzazu guy was plotting his next move. I could almost hear him.

Right on cue, there was a loud thud against my front door. I jumped at least a foot out of my chair. The Para, which I had just drawn out and then put away, materialized in my right fist again in the blink of an eye.

The door was struck again. Someone was definitely there. Someone serious about getting in. Fine, I told myself. Time to rock and roll. I stalked my way to the living room, prepared for action.

"Come out, come out, wherever you are!" I challenged them, throwing the door open and dropping down into a combat crouch, ready to blaze away.

Darkness greeted me. There was no one at the door. I frowned. That wasn't how this was supposed to go down. Zombies were stupid, single-minded automatons. They didn't play games or toy with their prey. Did they?

It occurred to me that I must look pretty stupid, crouched down in my doorway, drawing down on nobody. Better safe than sorry, I told myself. Someone had hit the door.

Curiosity got the better of me, and I eased forward to look outside. Just as I swiveled my head to the right, I heard a voice hiss, "Hey, asshole—over here!"

And there they were. Four members of the Chesapeake Bay Bloods. Or Crips. Or whatever the hell the local gang called themselves. I might as well refer to them as the JA-Nines, since all four of them were pointing those shitty handguns at me.

"What the fuck do you want?" I asked, reasonably enough, I thought. After all, I had been expecting the police first, and then the undead. The gang members hadn't even been on my radar.

"We want our money back, bro," a new voice answered, from my left. I shook my head in disappointment. I was really off my game. I hadn't noticed the fifth gangster.

"And if I say no?" Always the optimist.

"Then we kill you, torch your lame-ass crib, and take the money anyway," she replied.

There was a flaw in that reasoning, I thought. "Not to tell you your business, sister, but if you torch my house first, you'll have a hard time recovering the money. Just trying to help," I explained.

"You got a set of balls on you, bro. Maybe we do something about that, too, before we done here tonight," my new pal offered.

"No, thanks, I'll keep them where they are. The money, too. I need it for my mission." I didn't bother to explain what my mission was. No point in dragging the conversation down with unnecessary details.

"Man, screw your mission; that's our money. And we're getting it back, bro!" One of the other four rasped. I risked a glance back at him and smirked. It was the guy I'd hit in the throat with my AR. No wonder he sounded hoarse.

I was about to reply when there was a startled yelp from the leader. I twisted around to see what happened, and was just in time to see two ratty-looking corpses drag her to the ground. More were rushing up the driveway at me, and at least three or four had gotten behind my other friends to my right.

My first thought was, "Shit!" My second thought was that maybe if I went back inside and closed the door, my two adversarial groups would destroy each other, and I could enjoy the rest of the evening in peace.

As enticing as that thought was, I rejected it. Odds were, since both groups were here to get me, they'd either gang up on me, or one group would kill the other and then still go after me. Besides, the gang-bangers were morons and the dregs of society, but they were at least human. Mostly. They didn't deserve to be eaten by reanimated corpses.

"Get inside, now!" I barked, stepping fully outside of the door frame and motioning behind me. I didn't wait to see if anyone obeyed me or not; I had zombies to kill. The first three rounds dropped the wave rushing straight in. The next three took out the second wave. I felt scrambling behind me and to my right.

All four gang-bangers stumbled their way into my living room, leaving me outside alone to rescue their boss. I couldn't blame them. In fact, I'd told them to go inside, and they had. Good soldiers follow orders. It was my job to get their boss.

I risked a quick shot at the better of the two targets, and watched in satisfaction when it's head blew up, and the body collapsed like a puppet with its strings cut. The other one grabbed his victim's arm and chomped down.

The dealer screamed. I leaped forward and yanked the zombie's head back, forcing it to release the chick's arm. "Back to hell, shithead," I growled and put a round through its rotting skull.

I pulled the woman to her feet and turned back to my front door. We needed to get back inside; there were more undead streaming toward us. I used my last six shots to clear a path to the door, and shoved my way through the bodies, dragging my former enemy with me.

One of the others slammed the door shut behind us, and I dropped my burden to the floor. She groaned and held out her arm. "Fucking thing bit me," she said. Kinda obvious, I thought.

"What the hell are those things?" One of the others wanted to know.

"What the fuck do you think they are, bro? Motherfucking zombies. That's what they were," another said.

"Are you serious? Zombies? This is the real world, man, we don't have no zombies," the one that I'd previously hit in the throat shouted.

"No, man, I saw them. They was dead," the first one argued. "Freakin' zombies. With red fucking eyes."

All five looked at me, then. I'd let them ramble on while I grabbed a fresh magazine for the Para. I was reloaded now, and the threat was still out there. I nodded at the guns still held, forgotten, in their hands.

"Ain't over. They came to kill me, and you assholes got in the way. Guessin' you're on the menu, now, too. Any of you any good with those nines?"

All five blinked and looked at the guns clenched in their fists. A couple of them nodded. The one with the hurt throat looked back at me and scowled.

"So what now, asshole? You think we're gonna have your back or something? You gonna tell us what to do, whitebread?" I think he was still angry about catching the butt of my AR in the throat. Touchy.

"No need," I told him. "You can just leave. There's the door," I pointed. "Have a good night."

They exchanged looks. No one moved. Inwardly, I smirked. Outwardly, I showed nothing. Me and Clint Eastwood. Stone-faced Marines. Unflappable.

"No takers?" I asked after a time. "Okay, then listen the hell up. We need to..." I never got a chance to explain what I was sure was a brilliant plan, because at that moment the living room window exploded inward, glass spraying everywhere. The door was blasted open as well, and I could hear the back door in the kitchen being kicked in.

Zombies of every shape and size and degree of decay swarmed us. Their movements were frenzied, faster than I'd ever seen them. All of us humans condensed down to a tight circle in the middle of the living room, guns blazing.

"Aim for their heads!" I shouted, pretty sure that no one could hear me over the roar of all the gunfire. After initial panic firing, the drug goons figured it out on their own, though. They began to drop the zombies in their tracks, adding them to the growing pile that I was accumulating.

The air in the living room grew dense with gun smoke as the six of us tightened our circle and kept shooting. Problem was, it looked like there were more zombies than we had rounds. I heard swearing, and saw slides locking open as guns ran dry. I didn't see anyone slapping in fresh mags. I guess drug dealers didn't carry extra magazines.

It didn't matter. My pessimistic assessment turned out to be wrong. I took the last two down with my last four rounds. Silence reigned in my living room, except for the ringing in our ears. I peered through the haze from all the gunfire. There had to be at least thirty bodies strewn about. My house was shot to hell.

"Jesus Christ Almighty," one of the gang members said. He dropped his empty 9mm to the floor, and went to one knee. He appeared to be praying. I didn't know bad guys did that. Did he really think that God would listen to him, him being a bad guy and all?

My foray into philosophical whimsy was interrupted by Sgt. Bates. As always. The guy just wouldn't let me rest. *Get off your ass, Marine*, he growled in my ear. *There may be more. You gonna wait for the next wave or you gonna hit 'em back now?*

Bates was right. Again. I clambered over the inert corpses filling the living room and found my AR. After making sure it was loaded and racked, I stepped out into the darkness.

I didn't see anything or anyone lurking about. My neighbor wasn't home, either. That was probably for the best. Pretty sure he'd have been upset with the firefight on the lawn, and then the free for all in my living room. He might even have been hurt or killed. That would have sucked.

The idea that he would have called the cops flashed into my brain, too. Even if he'd been gone, someone on my street would have called in the shots fired by now. Which meant I was running out of time. I ducked back into what was left of my house.

And walked into an ongoing execution. Four of my new friends had their leader on the floor, and were about to put a bullet into her brain. She was arguing with them.

"Lemme go, you fuckers. You got no call to shoot me, dammit," she was saying as I walked in.

"Am I interrupting something?" I asked.

Without taking their eyes off of their former boss, they said, "She been bit. Gonna turn into one of them."

"You know that how?"

"Seen it in every one of them movies, dude. They always turn. That's how they take over. Ain't lettin' it happen here," raspy-voice told me, placing his gun on the back of his leader's head.

"Wait," I told him. "This isn't a damn movie. If it was, somebody cool would be playing me, and you'd be Denzel." I gave him a good stare. "Do you look like Denzel? I don't think so. Just hold off a minute."

I waved the others off. Leaning over, I asked the woman who'd been bitten, "You feeling like biting any of us?"

She glared up at me. I didn't blame her too much. I was being a prick. "Fuck you, bro," she spat.

"Never mind," I told the others. "Go ahead and kill her."

"Wait! I didn't mean nuthin', man, just chill. Don't let them shoot me," she said, changing her tune right on cue. Again, I smiled on the inside. Maybe there was more to that psychology crap than I'd thought. It was kinda fun.

"Well, I don't know, you guys were coming here to kill me..." I said, staring off into the distance.

"No way, bro, we was just gonna get our money back. Honest. How was we to know that you really had a mission, dude? I mean, this is what you meant, right? You fight these zombie things, right? For real?" She asked, genuinely enough. For a chick fighting to stay alive.

"Yeah. For real," I told her.

"Fucking A," she breathed. She looked me in the face for the first time. "Am I really gonna turn into one?"

I thought about what I'd just read about the manzazu and how he created his horde. I shook my head. "I don't think so. These zombies aren't from some virus. They're made by some fucking sorcerer guy." I looked at the others, still pointing their guns at the woman on the ground.

"I'm after this psycho, and he's tryin' to kill me with these dead people that he raises up. You gotta be dead before he can use you." I motioned at the girl on the floor. "She ain't gonna turn, unless she dies first."

"You sure, whitebread?" one of them wanted to know.

"No. Not sure of anything, really. But it's what I think. Keep an eye on her; you can always shoot her later, right?" I asked, looking back down at the her. She flinched, but kept her head up. A point for her.

"What's your name?"

"Shenzi," she told me.

"No, seriously. If I'm going to call off your boys, you can at least give me your name," I frowned at her.

"My name is Shenzi, bro. Wilson. Ask them," she said. I saw nods from the others.

"Okay," I shrugged.

I gave Shenzi a hand up, and motioned for her crew to give her back her empty gun. "Well, I'm guessing the cops are on the way. Probably not in any of our best interests to be here when they show up."

"No shit," one of them sneered.

"I can't leave the place this way," I said, looking around at all the bodies and mayhem. "This is gonna look bad."

"What do you suggest, bro, Merry Maids?" Shenzi asked, looking around with me. "Got any bright ideas?"

I nodded. "Actually, yeah. Let's do what you threatened to do earlier. Torch it. Guy on the other side of the duplex isn't home. Let's blow it up, burn it to the ground."

Shenzi looked surprised for a second; then nodded, too. Great minds think alike. "Maybe you ain't so dumb," she told me.

"Don't go all mushy on me, lady," I replied. "I'm still not giving you back your money."

"Keep it," she said. She stared at me, long and hard. A lifetime of tough choices and tougher circumstances showed in her eyes. "Yeah, keep it. You gonna need it. You fighting this kinda shit, you need more than that," she said, looking at her crew. They looked back steadily. "You need more, you find us. We'll work something out. This shit is wrong," she scowled, kicking at a corpse with her foot. "Fucked up beyond reason, bro."

"Yeah. It is," I said, my living room scene dissolving into the scene in Afghanistan, where my unit first encountered these zombies. "It truly is."

It took me less than two minutes to rearm and grab what I needed from the house. Three minutes later, just as the first sirens where audible in the distance, the duplex went up in flames.

CHAPTER 17

"Dude, you got a place to crash?" My newest and bestest buddy asked. I stared at the flaming ruins of my former residence and shook my head. I could see her stare at the flames as well. For a moment, we just stood there, side by side, fellow warriors in the fight against the undead.

For the first time in what seemed like years, I didn't feel alone. Someone else was there, knew what I knew, saw what I saw, and had my back. I stood a little straighter. Then Shenzi spoke again.

"Well, fuck this, man, we're outta here. This is some fucked up shit," she grumbled, turning her back to the fire and waving at her associates. "Let's get back to our job, selling shit, and leave this crazy fuck to his 'mission.'" So much for brotherhood in a common cause.

"I'd get scarce, too, bro," she told me. "Sounds like the cops are almost here. Good luck. Oh, yeah," she added. "You can keep the truck for now, too, man; you need it more than we do."

In seconds, they were gone, and I was alone. Again. I was a little bitter about that, but in retrospect, I couldn't blame them. They were just gang-bangers. Putting themselves in harm's way and risking their lives to save others wasn't part of their makeup. It's not like they were Marines. The few. The proud. The stupid and possibly delusional.

They were also right about getting out of the area. It was gonna get hot here, quickly, and not just from the fire. The sirens sounded like they were right on top of me. I jumped in my battered old truck and drove away, leaving the lights off for the first several blocks to avoid attention.

I needed a place to sleep, somewhere out of the way and cheap. Fortunately, there were no-tell motels and hotels on the other side of town; places where no one asked questions, and my migrant-worker pick up would look right at home. I headed that way.

An hour later, I dropped gratefully onto my sagging bed and closed my eyes. My new accommodations left a lot to be desired, like cleanliness and style, but they were home. Any port in a storm, I told myself and then snorted. Sounded like something a Navy guy would say. It wasn't like I was going to be bringing company here, anyway.

Not intentionally, I amended. Most of my recent company had been uninvited and unwelcome. Gang members trying to kill me, and zombies, also trying to kill me. My guest list needed improving. Once I got a new place, and this mess was over, I needed to find better friends.

I frowned. Almost asleep, my brain grabbed at the word *find*. It was no big deal for the gang guys to find me; it was their truck, and it was sitting in my driveway. But how did the zombies manage to find my house?

"Just because you're paranoid doesn't mean someone ain't out to get you," Sgt. Bates used to tell us. "You gonna be Force Recon Marines, you gotta expect the enemy to be after you."

I understood that. Even a dumb grunt like me could grasp basic concepts. Bad guys would try to get rid of us. Duh. My job was to get rid of them first. Problem was, they kept finding me. On my jog; out on the town; and now, at my damn house. How were they finding me? Was I GPS located or something? Tagged?

If I was, they'd be at my door again soon. It would be best to be prepared for that. I rolled out of my new bed.

My new quarters were even more difficult to secure, but I did the best I could, bracing the windows so that they couldn't be forced, stashing guns and knives in tactically-appealing locations, and generally zombie-proofing the place to within an inch of its life.

Feeling relatively secure, I spent the next three hours sleeping. After that, it was back to working out, first without weapons, and then with. Dry firing practice is nowhere near as much fun as live fire drills, but they are much less likely to draw unwanted attention to your hotel room. Even in a bad part of town.

In addition to being uncomfortable with the unsanitary conditions of my workout area, I felt awkward doing close quarters drills with my DPMS. The AR-15 was actually pretty handy in close quarters, but the entire time I was practicing, the rifle felt off somehow.

It felt...sulky. That was it. The damn rifle acted like it knew that I was comparing it in my mind to the Wilson Combat Recon sitting in Bill's office. Like a girl that knew she was on the verge of being dumped for someone else.

Not that I had a lot of experience with that sort of thing. Women were of tremendous interest to me, I just had very little experience with them, and they frightened me. Seriously. I had thought that becoming a kickass Marine would help curb my fear, but that hadn't happened.

Truth to tell, the Marines had taught me to be even more afraid of women. "You train for what the enemy can do, not what you think they'll do," Bates had told us, and every time that I saw a woman, I thought of all the undignified things that she could do to me.

And so, I kept my distance from women, and talked to my weapons. All they could do was kill me; they couldn't rip my still beating heart from my chest and eat it right in front of me. Of course, the zombies that were after me might do that. Some of them were female. Or had been, back when they were alive.

Forcing thoughts of the Wilson AR-15, and women, aside, I showered and ordered a pizza. "Man's gotta eat," I told my reflection in the mirror. "Can't solve the mysteries of the universe on an empty stomach." Besides, pepperoni was a basic food group, and when combined with melted cheese and the right crust, as close as a Marine could get to heaven.

After paying the delivery dweeb more than he deserved, I sat and stuffed my face. "Training be damned," I gloated, washing down the pizza with a two-liter of Dr. Pepper. I was fit enough to not worry about cholesterol and stuff like that. I even put salt on the stupid thing.

Twenty glorious minutes later, I leaned back and belched. The grease-coated cardboard lay empty in front of me. The two-liter bottle was on its side, crumpled in a ball. If an army really did travel on its stomach, I was ready.

I fought off the post-binge food coma, and once again tackled the problem of how the zombies were finding me. Surely now, fortified with the best that Pizza Hut had to offer, I could come up with the right answer.

After what seemed an eon or two, but couldn't have been more than half an hour in reality, I fired the balled up plastic bottle at the wall in disgust. "Fuck!" I yelled. "I really am too stupid to fall off a log. Damn, Bates was right all along," I grumbled, and could swear that I heard him chuckle back in the recesses of my mind. Prick.

"What am I missing? It's not like I've got a damn target painted on my back, or a sign on the door: human food, come right in." The room had no answer, and surprisingly, none of the voices in my head had any, either.

In the old days, when things were too complicated for a simple grunt like me, I could take my worries to an officer. Thinking was part of what officers were paid to do. Problem was, I had tried that route, and the Colonel had dumped it back in my lap.

I felt a little bit like maybe I was bait; held out by the Colonel or someone else, for the manzazu to keep trying for. Our unit had been used like that in Afghanistan, but that was different. I had the other guys to watch my back, and I had theirs. I was alone here.

Disgruntled and still tired, I gave in to my body's desire to crash. The mattress at my new digs was lumpy and uneven, but I'd slept on far worse, so it didn't keep me awake nearly as long as the thought of being stalked by the manzazu did.

I woke up grumpy. The pizza and Dr. Pepper from earlier hadn't settled well. I needed to get out. It was late, but early enough that a good run was still feasible.

The area the motel was in wasn't one that I was very familiar with, but as long as there were sidewalks and street lights, it should be fine, I told myself. In fact, it might even be safer, because no one knows where I am.

I put on my hoodie and grabbed the little Sig Sauer P938. Just in case there were lots of people out, I grabbed a cap and jammed it on my head, too. Make myself harder to recognize; at least for humans. I still had no idea how the zombies were finding me. Maybe it had nothing to do with seeing. Maybe they could smell me.

Surreptitiously, I sniffed under one arm. No BO. Maybe it was something else. I shrugged and started off. Having the gun in my fist was reassuring, but made me feel really self-conscious. I made sure to wave at the random other joggers with my other hand, or simply nod at them. Luckily there weren't a lot of them out in this neighborhood.

I normally set a decent pace for jogging, and tonight was no different. By decent, I mean I'm most comfortable with a seven-minute mile pace, and while I won't set any land speed records with it, it allows me to enjoy the scenery and keep a watchful eye out. It's pretty stupid to run so fast that you can't see or react to what's coming up next.

After fifteen minutes, my breathing evened out, the legs loosened up, and I actually started to enjoy myself. There's satisfaction in physical activity. The world starts to make sense, and problems seem to diminish. I just had to keep my eyes open for dead guys trying to make me dead, too. No biggie.

Half an hour later, the world intruded into my run. Not the monstrous, supernatural world of the manzazu and his minions, but the simple, bad side of Chesapeake, where stupid things happen because there are stupid people there.

I was pounding along, minding my own business, when I came around a corner and right in front of me was some asshat dragging a woman down the front steps of a house by her hair. She didn't seem to be enjoying it very much. The guy was explaining the facts of life to her.

"Bitch, you are going with me. I own your dumb ass, and you know it," he was shouting. She was screaming back at him, but I couldn't understand anything except the word "no" somewhere in the middle.

I made to swerve out of the way and keep going. It wasn't my problem, and people fight all the time. I couldn't change that. I wasn't some Boy Scout. Nor was I some superhero, out to rescue damsels in distress.

About the same time that they reached the sidewalk, I reached them. The guy looked up at me and sneered. "The fuck you lookin' at?" He asked. I sighed, and stopped running. I put my hands on my hips and breathed.

"Well?" The guy insisted. "You better just keep goin', faggot, before you get hurt."

I looked at him. "First of all, no one uses the term 'faggot' anymore; it's not politically correct. Keep up with the times, dick. Second of all, maybe I just stopped to see your dating techniques. I'm single myself, and thought you could give me some pointers. I kinda thought the 'dragging them off to your lair by the hair' thing went out with the cavemen, though."

He let go of the woman. "Stay there, bitch; if you know what's good for you," he told her, and then stepped toward me. He brought his hands up in front of him and assumed some kind of martial arts stance. "Let's see how funny you are after I kick your teeth in, asshole!"

I smirked. I figured most men that beat on women were stupid; it was nice to see my theory proven right. I feinted with my left hand high, and then stepped in with my right and laid the barrel of the Sig alongside his nose.

The guy froze, his eyes crossing as he tried to look at the gun that had appeared in his face like magic. It was comical. I felt like saying, "ta da!," but that would have been too much, so I settled for "I wouldn't, shithead." Almost as good. All in all, I was feeling pretty good.

And that's when I sensed movement behind me, and felt a burning sensation in my lower back. I yelled and spun around, knocking an arm up in the air with my gun hand as I turned.

"Leave him alone!" The woman shrieked and swung at me again with the bloody knife in her hand.

I couldn't move back, since there was already an asshole behind me waiting to kick my teeth in, so I sidestepped left, slapping the knife past me and putting some distance between me and the pair of crazies.

"What the hell was that for? I was trying to help you," I rasped, trying to decide whether or not to shoot both of them. Him, for being an abusive asshole, and her for stabbing me in the back. I decided that I couldn't do it.

"Never mind. Just get the hell out of here. Now. If you even look at me funny, I will shoot both of you," I told them, and waved toward the street. The couple glanced at each other, looked at me and the cocked semi auto pistol in my hand, and moved off. They got into a much nicer car than they had any right to own, and drove off.

Once they were out of sight, I lowered my gun and slumped. I reached across and touched my right side with my left hand. It came away covered in blood. I looked down and immediately wished that I hadn't. It hurt now. A lot.

I figured that I was five miles from my hotel room. There was no way I could make it that far. Already, my vision was getting a little blurry. I peered around, hoping that maybe my new friends the honeymooning couple had come back and wanted to give me a ride. No such luck.

I shook my head, trying to clear my vision, and started walking. Five miles wasn't so far. I'd gone farther than that with a bullet in me once, in Afghanistan. This was just a little cut, from a freaking girl. No big deal.

I stumbled on, focusing on putting one foot in front of the other. It seemed to be getting darker, but that wasn't possible, it should be getting lighter, right? I wondered vaguely if I was losing too much blood, and turned around to look and see if I was leaving a trail. At least, I thought I turned around. I had an impression of spinning, and then falling. I heard a dog bark, pretty close to me, and then things went out of focus, so I closed my eyes.

CHAPTER 18

I HEARD VOICES MURMURING. That wasn't unusual. In fact, it was the new normal. There were almost always voices in my head, lecturing me, telling me all of the things that I was doing wrong.

These voices were different, though. I didn't recognize them. I frowned. The voices seemed to get excited at this.

"Doctor, I think he's coming around," a decidedly female voice said. I grimaced at that; most of the voices in my head were masculine. On the other side of my head, another voice responded.

"I think you're right. It's about time, too. I was starting to get worried," a severe, know-it-all type growled. The tone pissed me off, so I opened my eyes to see what he looked like.

I squinted and tried to focus. For some reason, everything looked as blurry to my eyes as the voices sounded in my ears. I shook my head in order to clear it.

Soft hands clasped the sides of my skull, and the feminine voice said, "Hey, relax, honey. Try not to move around, okay? You're groggy from the medications that are in your system. It'll pass, just give it some time."

I did as ordered and lay still. The woman took one hand away, and gently patted me on the forehead with the other. "That's a good boy. Do you know where you are?"

A face leaned over me, and the image cleared enough to reveal a compassionate-looking woman in scrubs, smiling at me upside down. I cleared my throat.

"Hospital?"

She beamed like I'd won a spelling bee or something. "That's right. You're at the hospital. You were stabbed. You lost a lot of blood, but you're going to be fine, okay? So don't worry about anything," she assured me, continuing to pat my head.

Stabbed? I was stabbed? I've been at war with the undead, I wanted to tell her. Zombies don't use knives. Or do they? My head was starting to ache, so I shut my eyes again and let my mind go blank. With the help of the anesthesia, it was pretty easy to do.

Just as I was about to drift off completely, I heard footsteps and then a new voice. This one sounded familiar.

"Where is Chase Brooks? I was told that he was here. I'm here to supervise his transfer to the VA," Doctor Sovers demanded. His voice got louder as he got closer to my gurney. "There you are, Brooks. Always into something, aren't you? Well, you can relax for now. I'm here to take care of you," he said.

"Doc Sovers...did I miss a meeting or something?" I managed to croak. "They said I got stabbed, why are you here? Did I get stabbed in the brain?" For some reason that seemed really funny to me, so I giggled. Undignified, but I blame the meds.

The shrink wasn't nearly as amused. "Mr. Brooks, I don't know what you were out doing when you suffered your injury, but I doubt that you were the victim of an unprovoked attack, and I'm positive that there is nothing here to make light of. I'm also certain that Colonel LeMasters would agree."

Images flew though my brain as the doc spoke. First, I saw myself running, a gun clenched in my right hand. Then, a quick vision of some jerk dragging a woman outside by her hair. I saw myself interceding, and then getting stabbed in the back by the woman I stopped to protect. And then the rest of Sovers' words penetrated my thick skull.

"The Colonel?" I asked, trying to get up. Hands quickly pushed me back down.

"You stay down, Mr. Brooks. You're in no condition to start walking around. The surgeon just finished stitching you back together; let's not ruin all his fine work, okay?" Sovers said, almost kindly. He must have been showing off for the nurse. She had seemed cute, although that could have been the meds, too.

"I need to see the Colonel," I informed them. "It's important."

"Later, Chase, for right now, you just rest," the nurse whispered. "It'll all be okay. We're moving you to the VA so you can get better. You must be very important, to warrant your doctor coming here so quickly to take charge of your recovery." She patted me again. Despite her intentions, it was starting to annoy me.

"Look, nurse, I'm not a dog."

She leaned in and looked at me, confused. "I don't understand, Chase. What do you mean, you're not a dog? Your doctor is not a veterinarian; he's a people doctor."

Oh my God, I thought. My nurse thinks I'm an idiot. Join the club, I mentally told her. The line forms to the left. As clearly as I could, I explained. "No. Doctor Sovers is a shrink, so he isn't a vet or a people doctor, really."

I paused a moment to get my breath. Who knew that talking was so tiring? "And I'm not a damn dog, so stop petting my head, okay? You're making my headache worse," I told her.

The patting stopped immediately. I swore the temperature dropped thirty degrees in less than two seconds. "Well, we wouldn't want to make you any worse, now, would we?" She huffed. I felt her move back.

"Doctor Reynolds, should we get the patient moved out of here right away, like Doctor Sovers requested? We are transferring him to his care, after all," she said, rather coldly.

"What did I do?" I mumbled, trying to figure out the sudden

turn. I really don't understand women. I should just count this exchange as an improvement, though, I told myself as she threw a bag with my belongings on my legs, along with my chart. The last woman I'd seen had stabbed me.

I really didn't want to be helpless and under the doc's care. I tried to sit up and explain that to my formerly helpful nurse, but she ignored my pleas and even assisted in strapping me down on the bed so that I couldn't move. The bastards told me that it was for my own protection.

If it was really for my protection, they'd have given me my Sig back. Speaking of which... "Hey, where is my gun? I had a little 9mm when I went out for my run. I want it back."

The nurse actually snorted. "You're in the hospital with IV lines running into your arms, naked, still under the influence of pain killers, possibly dangerous, and you want your gun? Fat chance, buddy."

"A little professionalism, Nurse Williams. Mr. Brooks here is a combat veteran, and feels distinctly at risk without his firearms," Sovers reprimanded. He leaned over my bed and smirked.

"Your precious gun is safe, Mr. Brooks. You still had it in your hand when you were admitted to the ER. I'm told it had to be pried out of your hand, even unconscious. I have it, separate from your clothing. It will go with us to the VA." He started to turn away but leaned back in and added, "I will have Sergeant Paxton unload it and keep it safe."

Bastard. Way to hit me where it hurts. I lay still (not like I had a choice) and quiet (my choice to sulk) as they wheeled me out through the ER doors and to an ambulance. Once there, two dark complexioned guys put me in the back and slammed the doors.

The ambulance rolled out of the parking lot without the flashing lights. Idly, I wondered why I didn't rate the lights, and then decided that it didn't matter. Bored, I looked around at the inside of the ambulance. It was very quiet in the ambulance, the paramedics didn't seem inclined to talk, and they didn't play the radio.

I frowned. It *was* quiet. Too quiet. There were no voices in my head. Normally, I could count on at least one of them for company when the world got too quiet. It was almost enough to make me paranoid.

Finally, one of the guys up front spoke. "Is this our only service call?" He asked his partner.

"Yeah, I think so. I can check with dispatch," the other replied. In the back, I frowned again. Both men had accents. Middle Eastern.

I'm not a prejudiced person. Never have been. Don't plan on ever being one. At the same time, I'd served my country overseas, and been shot at by people with that same accent, and now, back in my own country, was being stalked by some mystic who undoubtedly had the same accent, too. I instinctively disliked these two.

Screw this, I told myself. Time to get out of these restraints. I know that hospitals take pride on their soft restraint systems, and teach new nursing assistants and paramedics how impossible it is to get out of them, but they're wrong.

It took me less than three minutes to take the straps off of my chest and legs. I figured it took a little longer than it should have because I had to be quiet. The residual meds in my system probably didn't help, either.

The medics hadn't noticed. They'd been playing games with the radio. Now that I was free to concentrate, I could hear them conversing.

"Why do we have to pick up another body? That's like all we do now."

"We've always picked up stiffs, it goes with the job. You know that."

"This is different. Since *he* showed up, we've doubled our service calls for picking up corpses. And they're never from nursing homes, do you notice that? It makes me wonder," the passenger seat guy said.

The driver shook his head. "Better that you don't think about it. Just do your job and keep your head down. He won't be around forever."

"It's not right. We're American citizens now. He has no right to do this to us," the first one insisted. "We don't have to be afraid of him anymore."

"Fine. You tell him that. I'm certain that he'll understand."

I swore that I could feel the passenger shudder. Despite the thickness of their accents, I had no trouble hearing the fear in their voices. Whoever they were talking about scared the shit out of them.

Whatever. I had problems of my own. They could solve theirs by themselves. At least, that's what I told myself as we pulled into the ER at the VA. And then, out of nowhere, I heard the passenger mutter, "fucking manzazu. Just die already, and leave us alone."

My heart had to have stopped when the paramedic dropped his bomb. Despite his thick accent, I knew that I'd heard him correctly. The son of a bitch had actually said "manzazu." There was no mistake.

I sat upright, fast enough to make my head swim. I couldn't afford to let a little nausea slow me down; these assholes were working for my arch enemy. I swept the blanket off of me and swung my feet down to the floor.

Then two things happened at the same time. The back doors of the ambulance opened, and I glanced down to see that I was completely naked. Dizzy I could ignore. Naked was a different matter. Guess I would have made a rotten Spartan. I heard that they used to fight naked. Not me. I snatched the blanket back up just in time, as the two paramedics and a female nurse poked their heads in the back of the ambulance.

"What is the patient doing sitting up? You guys know better than that. This is totally unacceptable," the nurse snapped, pushing the men aside and jumping in with me. Before I could even think to protect myself, she shoved me back down on the gurney and strapped me back in.

Turning back to the paramedics, she growled, "This patient could have been seriously injured, riding in the back of an ambulance unstrapped. And for the record, one of you should have been riding in the back with him. I believe that is policy when transporting live patients, is it not?"

When the two men just shuffled their feet and looked like school kids caught being bad, she clucked her tongue at them and yelled for help from the direction of the ER doors. It didn't take long. Apparently this woman ran the show at the VA Emergency Room. God knows I was intimidated by her.

While being wheeled into the hospital, I twisted around as best I could to read the side of the ambulance. I had to know who those guys were. "City Ambulance Service," I read aloud. Not very original. At least I was out of their hands.

"Mr. Brooks, welcome back to the VA," Sovers greeted me, once inside. "I have a nice room all ready for you," he said, all smug as hell.

Talk about out of the frying pan and into the fire. I'd have been better off with the crooked ambulance crew, I told myself. At least I could have tried pumping them for intel. There was nothing to gain from being incarcerated with this hack...unless...

"So, doc, you gonna tell the Colonel on me?"

Sovers looked down at me, eyes squinting like he was trying to read my mind. "Why would I bother a busy man like Colonel LeMasters with an unimportant event like this? He has more pressing matters than visiting your bedside after getting into yet another scrape and getting stabbed for your poor decision-making," Sovers lectured. The asshole. He didn't even know how I'd gotten hurt, and yet here he was, blaming me for everything.

"Good," I told him. "I don't want the Colonel to know anything about this," I sniffed, turning away as much as the restraints would allow. "I wouldn't talk to him anyway." Maybe reverse psychology would work. I knew Sovers wouldn't knowingly help me out.

"We'll see, Chase. For now, it's important that you rest. It's way too early to think about bothering the Colonel, anyway," Sovers said smoothly, not taking the bait. So, he was an asshole, but he was a smart asshole. Damn it.

It wasn't that big a shock that I'd failed to outsmart a doctor. He should be smarter than I am; he's a college graduate and all that, and I'm just a kick-ass Marine. So if guile didn't work, I should just go with my strengths...if I could figure any out.

I was silent on the trip to my new room at the VA. As they were hooking everything up I looked around. It looked a lot like the last room I was in while at the VA.

"Well, there we are, Mr. Brooks. All settled. You rest, and we'll talk later on. I should be able to rearrange my schedule to see you late morning at some point. We'll talk about what happened to you. I'm afraid that the police may have to be involved, but we'll cross that bridge when we get there, right?" Sovers said, not really paying attention to whether I agreed or not. I think he just liked to hear the sound of his own voice. Like most shrinks, I suppose.

The good doc swept out of my room, dropping my file in the tray on the wall next to the door. I thought about trying to leave right away, but gave up on that idea as soon as I tried to sit up. Who knew that getting stabbed and losing a gallon or two of blood would make you so dizzy and weak?

I knew one thing, though: I didn't want to be around when the police showed up. That would complicate my mission. Somehow, I'd avoided their involvement so far, and I needed that to continue.

I was still plotting and planning ways to get out, and what I'd tell the police if and when they finally showed up when I dropped off to sleep.

CHAPTER 19

Colonel LeMasters was sitting next to my bed when I woke up. The scene was starting to feel too familiar. He must have thought the same thing, judging by the expression on his face.

"Morning, sir," I said.

"Good morning, Brooks. I wasn't expecting to see you again so soon; especially here," he said, smiling slightly.

"Same," I muttered.

"At least you're in better shape than the last time you showed up here."

"Yeah," I replied.

"Dr. Sovers says that you should be out of here in no time. If you behave yourself," LeMasters said.

I nodded, staring at the wall.

"All right, Brooks, out with it. What's wrong? Other than having a new hole in your side," he demanded.

"Sir," I said, turning to look at him. "Why the hell was Sovers at the other hospital? I understand some kid walking her dog found me in the street and called for an ambulance. How and why would my damn shrink be at the hospital?"

LeMasters smiled at me. "Is that all? It isn't that complicated, Brooks, and nothing nefarious. When you were shipped here from Afghanistan, you had no family listed. We had Dr. Sovers listed as your emergency contact on your chart. The hospital ER saw your dog tags and looked you up. They called here right away, and were referred to the doc."

I frowned. "Great. He's my emergency contact. Like family," I grumbled. "Swell."

"Just look at him as that creepy uncle that every family has," the Colonel grinned. "One that knows all your dirty laundry and secrets. Anything else, young man?"

"Yeah. Why no cops? Not just with the attacks, but when I got stabbed? Doesn't every stab wound and every gunshot wound at an ER get called in to the cops? I expected to be interviewed by the cops the second I woke up," I told him.

The Colonel's grin disappeared and a frown took its place. "I don't know. Usually that's the case, I believe. You should ask Dr. Sovers; I think he's handled all of those matters.

"Well, I have other things that need my attention," he said, getting to his feet. "You get better, and we'll talk more real soon. I can tell by the look on your face that you have more to tell me, but it will have to wait for another time. See you, Brooks," he waved and walked out.

He was right; there was much to tell him. I hadn't told him about the fight at my house and its subsequent torching, or the ambulance drivers. But if he didn't have time, he didn't have time. We'd catch up later. In the meantime, I needed out.

Once I ate my breakfast, took my pain meds, and sent the nurse from the room, I found my clothes, put them on, even if they were stiff with crusted blood, and headed out the door.

"Mr. Brooks!" A gravelly voice called. I stopped, and turned my head. At the nurse's station was the ugliest troll I'd ever seen; arms folded in disapproval, head shaking, with a severe expression on its face.

"Mr. Brooks, I don't know where you think that you're going, but Doctor Sovers has certainly not released you from this hospital. Is there something that I can help you with?"

Not likely, I snorted. Even if I was staying, which I wasn't. "No, thanks anyway," I mumbled, and resumed walking. The troll leveraged herself up and out from behind the desk. Her intentions were clear. She meant to keep me from leaving.

Not happening. The Corps was leaving, and no obstacle, no matter how large or resolute, was going to prevent that. "I am in fact leaving. If there's something that I need to sign, I will, otherwise, it's been real," I informed her.

She didn't seem impressed. One meaty hand reached out and clamped onto my arm. Despite the flab, and the dubious femininity of the nurse, her grip was like iron. Maybe I wasn't as recovered as I thought. I twisted and pulled my arm free.

"Look lady, no offense, but I have things to do. And they don't include you."

"Mr. Brooks, Doctor Sovers left specific instructions that you were not to leave the hospital without his approval. I believe that the police were also interested in talking with you about the nature of your injury," she huffed, trying to get back in front of me.

I sidestepped, enjoying the difference in our mobility. "It isn't up to Doctor Sovers, and if the police had wanted to talk to me, they could have done so at any time during the past twenty-four hours. If they stop by, be sure and give them my address; the doc has it."

The nurse had one more card to play, and she played it just as I was about to round the corner and open the door to the stairs. "Ahem. Perhaps you weren't paying very much attention to your clothes while you were getting dressed, Mr. Brooks. In addition to your sweats being covered in dried blood, did you happen to notice that they are cut all the way up, in front and in the back?"

I froze again, like we were playing red light—green light. I glanced down, and saw that she was right. "What the hell..."

"Standard procedure when someone comes in to the ER injured

and incapacitated, Mr. Brooks. The clothes are cut away from the injured area, so that it can be worked on. Frankly," she smirked, "I'm amazed that they bothered to save them at all."

She waddled in front me, and pointed back toward my room. Apparently she thought that she'd won. She didn't know me very well. I peered at her badge.

"Look, Christie...I'm leaving. Around you or over. I learned in the Corps that women are no different than men if they're in the way. And if you think that I'll be too embarrassed to walk out of here in cut up clothes, covered in blood, you never saw me during basic; I practically lived that way. So," I continued, reaching out to move her to the side.

"So, out of my path, or under it, nurse."

She glared at me, and I stood toe to toe with her, glaring back. She had me by fifty pounds or so, but I was a foot taller, and in better fighting trim. After what seemed like ten minutes, but was probably only a few seconds, she muttered, "fuck it," and turned to the side.

Who says I don't have a way with women? "Thank you, Nurse Christie; you're one in a million. Tell Doc Sovers that I said good bye." I signed the discharge papers at the nurse's station under the angry and petulant glare of the troll, slowly and with a flourish.

I dropped the pen on the desk, smirked, and walked out. Out of the ward, down the stairs, into the lobby, and out into the glorious sunshine. I pretended to be oblivious to the startled looks that my appearance caused.

Once out on the sidewalk, I paused. My escape from the hospital was complete, but it occurred to me that not only was I wearing cut up and bloodied clothing, but I also had no ride. Or money to get a cab or catch a bus. Or friend to call to come pick me up.

Sometimes being an army of one sucks. So I resigned myself to an entire day of hoofing it, dressed like an extra from a horror movie. It wasn't too bad. Walking was simple, and gave me plenty of opportunity to think.

The walk was going better than expected; the stitches were tight but not painful, and I was pretty pleased with myself. And that's when I noticed a red Toyota Camry with tinted windows, rolling really slowly on the street beside me. I had no idea how long it had been there; I'd been lost in La-la Land and proud of it.

The passenger side window started to roll down, and I swore. Nothing like being an easy target. I stopped and crouched, ready to spring to the side if I saw a gun barrel poke out.

"Relax, dude. If I wanted you greased, you would have been," a familiar voice called. Shenzi leaned out the open window, looking amused. "Whatsa matter, bro, afraid somebody's gonna knock you off for a fashion violation?"

I relaxed. Mostly. "Shut up. What are you doing, out and about during daylight? Aren't you supposed to be one of the walking dead by now?"

Shenzi looked worried for a moment. "Not yet, man. My arm kinda itches, though, ya know? Got it checked out. Cleaned the wound, got a bunch of damn shots. Hurt like a bitch," she grumped. I saw her motion the driver, and the car slid over to the curb.

I stepped over a little closer. Not quite in stabbing range, but close enough to make a move if my new buddy had second thoughts on offing me. My record with "friends" was spotty at best.

"Hey, come here," Shenzi called, quietly. She hung her head down, like she was shy or uncomfortable. "Man, I owe you. My crew was gonna waste me, you know, after...you know."

I shrugged. I was never eloquent when people were praising or thanking me. Luckily, that kind of thing didn't happen very often. "No problem. Didn't seem necessary."

Shenzi looked me up and down. "So, zombie slayer, what the hell happened to you, anyway? You almost get wasted by some of your enemies, like the other night?"

I shook my head this time. My range of expressions was amazing. Me and Kristen Stewart. "Not this time," I grumbled, hoping that she'd let it go. She didn't.

"Then what? Don't tell me it was some kitchen accident, either, man," Shenzi asked. "You may be unsafe, but you ain't THAT unsafe. Besides," she chuckled. "You ain't got no kitchen no more."

I sighed. "No. I got stabbed in the back by some chick I was trying to protect. Shoulda known better. Asshole was dragging her down the stairs, I had a problem with it, and she stabbed me from behind. Okay?"

Shenzi seemed amused. Which made me want to punch her. I didn't, of course; I knew she had back up, and they were probably armed. And I wasn't; no one would give me back my little Sig. I missed that gun. Especially right now.

"Bro, you gotta watch women. They're more dangerous than zombies. Don't trust 'em. Ever," Shenzi announced. Like she was some kinda genius.

"Thanks. I'll remember that." I went to move off, but she raised a hand.

"Yo, whitebread, you want a ride? Save you some wear and tear on that injury. Can't have our knight broken," she said. The back door opened.

I considered my options. I could spend several hours walking back to my rat-trap hotel, or catch a ride with gang-bangers that just last week had wanted me dead. Life was interesting sometimes.

"Fuck it," I said, unconsciously repeating what Nurse Christie had said when she let me leave. I bent down and slid into the back of the car almost sitting on the guy with the hoarse voice from the other night.

He glared daggers at me. Maybe Shenzi was okay with me, but this guy clearly wasn't. I smiled really big at him to show that there were no hard feelings. He grudgingly moved over, and I slammed the door shut.

"Where to, whitebread?" Shenzi asked.

"The Hill Top, off White Avenue," I told him. She snorted.

"Dude, you living high on the hog. We don't even deal there, man. Got lower lifes than us to handle that shithole." She nodded at the driver, who pulled out into traffic and set off toward my palace.

I spent the ride staring back at the man that I'd hit in the throat with the butt end of my AR. He spent the trip telling me with his eyes that he hadn't forgotten that moment, either. It was altogether an unpleasant journey, but much better than walking would have been.

CHAPTER 20

My hotel room looked just like it had when I left it, which was sad. I had been hoping that somehow it had been transformed into something nice while I was away. No such luck. At least it wasn't any worse.

I took a hot shower, and dressed in fresh, uncut, unbloodied clothes. I put on my in-the-waistband holster and stuck my trusty Para into it. An extra magazine was slipped into a pocket, along with my flashlight, and two knives were hidden away in various places.

Satisfactorily armed, I looked up the address of the City Ambulance Service, grabbed the keys to my truck, and headed back out the door. Zombies wait for no man. There was no telling what they had been up to during my vacation.

In under twenty minutes there I was, sitting in the parking lot at City Ambulance. It was less than impressive. Looked a lot like a crappy cab stand, or a seedy shipping company. City Ambulance obviously wasn't raking in the dough.

I sat, just taking in the ambiance for half an hour. There didn't seem to be anything going on. The parking lot had a couple vehicles in it that weren't in any better shape than my truck. At least it helped me blend in better.

Finally, an ambulance pulled in. I sat up in my seat. The ambulance lurched to a stop, and the same two guys that drove me around got out. They looked pretty tired. Maybe they worked around the clock.

I knew some EMTs, and they mostly worked twelve-hour shifts. These guys looked like they'd done several straight twelve-hour rotations. Like they hadn't been off shift since they took me to the VA.

Whatever, I told myself. They're tired, I'm tired. Everybody's tired. Let's get going. So I stepped out of my truck and raised my hand. My blending in to the background ploy had worked better than I'd intended; they ignored me entirely.

"Hey!" I called. That worked. They jumped a foot off the ground and spun in my direction. That was better. "Hey, I need to talk to you two for a minute. You took me to the hospital a couple days ago, remember?"

They looked at me blankly for a minute, but then they seemed to recognize me. Maybe I'm taller and look different standing up. And conscious.

"What do you want?" The stockier one asked, with the thick accent that I remembered from that night. "We don't know anything. We just answer the call, and pick up patients."

The other guy nodded, but his eyes shifted away. Maybe it was just discomfort at being questioned by someone as big as both of them put together, or maybe they had something to hide.

I tried for tact. "What the hell is going on here? I heard you that night; you were talking about the manzazu. I want him." For a Marine, that *was* tactful. For anyone else on the planet, it might have been considered rude and unsubtle.

My method didn't work on these two. The stockier one scowled and cut loose with a string of Afghani that I'm certain was mostly profane, and the shifty-eyed one made a move like he was pulling a weapon.

I stifled the urge to draw, and held up both hands. "Relax, boys. I just want to talk. I know that you don't like the guy. I don't like him either, but it's important that I find him." I smiled. *That should help*, Bates snickered. *You were always the pretty one.*

"Shut up!" I snapped. Both guys looked at me, puzzled, and I realized that I had answered Bates out loud. I shook my head. Damn drill sergeant. Back to my interrogation.

"How do you know the manzazu? Where is he right now? Why the hell is he here, anyway?" I growled. Smiling hadn't worked, maybe being intimidating would.

At my worst, I have been considered very intimidating. Downright scary. I must have been this time, too. The two paramedics bolted. A small knife clattered on the asphalt as they turned and ran to the business's front door.

"Hey," I shouted, and took off after them. They beat me to the front door, flew inside, and locked me out. I must be getting slow. Or maybe they just caught me off guard by taking off so quickly. Either way, I felt pretty stupid, standing outside the door of this business, with two guys looking through the glass at me, eyes wide with fear, but still slightly mocking.

I resisted the urge to put my elbow through the glass. That wouldn't help my cause. I needed to try a different route. I tried looking forlorn and sad. Didn't work. I took out a piece of paper and held it up, like it was official and something that they needed to see. That didn't work, either.

Finally, I shrugged, waved at my scaredy-cat prey, and made a show of giving up. I walked back to the truck, got in, and drove off. After two blocks, I whipped into an alley and threw out anchor.

I hustled out of the truck and sprinted (lumbered, in reality) back to City Ambulance. They wouldn't be dumb enough to just unlock the front door, but maybe they would relax enough to NOT go and check the back door. I ducked into the back alley, figured out where City Ambulance's back door should be, checked for security cameras, and then pulled on the door.

It opened. Uncle Sam loves his Misguided Children, and apparently God does, too. I crept through a dark hallway, past a dingy kitchen, a couple offices, and came up on my two EMT buddies still staring out the front glass. A moderately cute receptionist-type was standing behind them, also peering out into the parking lot.

"Do you think he's still out there?," the slimmer man asked.

"He left in his truck, Rafiq. He's not out there anymore," the stockier guy replied. "Unless he parked somewhere and came back, but why would he do that?"

This seemed like a good place to reintroduce myself. "Maybe so I could slip in the back. I did say that I really needed to talk to you guys," I announced, standing just out of reach behind them.

They jumped at least a foot. I was far too cool to laugh out loud, but I did allow myself a smirk. I could do covert when I had to. They'd been so focused on watching out the door for me, I think that I could have walked up and put my arm around them both. Not that I would have; I'm much too cool for that, too.

The slightly larger one balled his hands into fists and moved in front of the receptionist. A point for him. The smaller one reached in his pocket for his knife, and then froze as he remembered that it was lying in the parking lot from the last time we'd met. I smiled.

"You can relax, dude. I wouldn't hurt the lady. Not really interested in hurting you, either. I just want some answers."

"We don't know anything," the bigger guy muttered, keeping his hands up. Apparently he wasn't overly reassured by my words. I hate it when people don't believe me; makes me feel like they're judging me in the negative.

You did just sneak into the back of their business, Lieutenant Rodriquez reminded me. *And most Afghani people distrusted the Marines,* he added. *You gotta win their trust, not just demand it. Not just be covert, then, but charismatic.*

I paused. I was never as good at winning friends and influencing people as I was at breaking down doors. If I had people skills I would have been an officer.

"Gentlemen, everything is going to be okay. No one is in trouble. I just need to ask you guys some questions about shit...I mean, stuff that I heard you talking about the other night in your ambulance. Look," I said, pulling out the smaller EMT's blade. "Look, I picked up your knife in the parking lot. You can have it back," I offered, holding the little folder out to him.

"Rafiq, right?" I asked when he took it from me. He looked up, nodded, and put the blade back into his pocket. "I really do just want to talk."

The other guy lowered his fists. He didn't move any closer, but I sensed a slight lessening of tension in the room. Damn, the Louie was right. Maybe I should listen to him more. And trust my own instincts less. At least when it came to dealing with other people.

"The other night, you guys took me from one hospital to another. On the way, you were talking about the manzazu. Tell me about him," I asked.

They visibly tensed right back up at the mention of the manzazu. *Good going, dickhead,* Bates grumped. *Now they'll tell you everything.*

I tried again. "Look, I know what the manzazu is. He's attacked me four times in the last week. For whatever reason, he's after me. I need intel, and you guys know him. And I know that you don't like him."

Both men looked at the floor. The receptionist shifted her weight nervously, and glanced at the two, but didn't speak. She at least looked like she was paying attention. I addressed her for the first time.

"Hey, lady, you look like someone who cares about others. I'm betting that you started working here to help other people, didn't you? Well, people are dying out there. This manzazu piece of shit is to blame. And he isn't going to stop. Help me stop him," I begged, giving her the sad puppy-dog eyes that always work for me.

She stared into my eyes for a long moment, sighed, and sat down in a chair. "What do you want to know?" She asked. The two EMTs protested, and she waved them down.

"He's right," she told them. "We cannot go on like this. I don't want to live like my parents did. I will not live in fear, and continue to be a part of his evil; it poisons my soul."

The stockier man was shaking his head, scowling. "Abas, you know that she is right. You said the same thing to me just a few days ago, while we were transporting this one," Rafiq said, pointing at me. "You said these very words. We need to cleanse ourselves of this sin, before it follows us into the next life."

I'd let them go on, since talking wasn't my strong suit. But the inactivity was getting to me. I grabbed a chair, and slid it over to Rafiq, kicking another toward Abas at the same time. They jumped a little at the sudden movements, but recovered quickly. Rafiq sat in his, turning it to face me. Abas stood, ignoring the chair, and glaring at me.

"Abas, right? Just help me out. No one is asking you to get involved. You don't have to fight this guy, or take on the zombie horde all alone or anything. Just give me the right tools to put a stop to this shit. Sit down and talk with me," I said, and turned a fourth chair around and sat in it backward. I always liked sitting in folding chairs that way, made me feel like I could spring into action faster.

"Ma'am, what's your name? How do you know this guy?" I asked, looking back to the receptionist.

"Stop calling him a 'guy.' He is a monster. An abomination under God," Abas growled, cutting me off. He pushed his chair forward and sat heavily in it. Apparently he had made up his mind to talk. About time.

"The manzazu is beyond you, Marine. He is timeless, evil from ages ago, refusing to die. His powers come from hell itself, and you cannot stop him. Even with our help, you will not succeed. Many have tried before," he started, his voice low. I wondered how he knew that I was a Marine, but then remembered that he would have heard the nurses, and my good friend Dr. Sovers, talking about me.

"My father tells stories of his father and others in our village, rising up, attacking the manzazu's fortress in the hills, and trying to save our village from his evil. They failed. Only my grandfather and two others even returned that night," Abas said. Rafiq flinched at the last thing that was spoken. Abas noticed, and held up a hand.

"I misspoke. The others came home, also. Three nights later. My father said that three days after the raid, during the full moon, the nine men who died trying to end the manzazu returned to the village. They returned to their homes, and their loved ones," Abas said. His voice was bitter. "And they tore them to shreds."

The receptionist shuddered. She lifted her head, and tears were in her eyes. "My mother tells this story. She was just a little girl. Her father was one of those cursed beings that returned. When he entered their house, his eyes were lit with unholy fires, burning red. My grandmother ran to him, overjoyed at his return. He caught her in his arms, and tore out her throat in front of their child, my mother.

"My mother went out the window, and ran through the village, trying to get help. All around her, screams and shouting. It seems that the other men did the same thing upon their return," she said, her voice carefully neutral; matter of fact.

I wasn't fooled. I knew she was close to losing it. So I distracted her. I coughed, and looked at Rafiq. He hadn't told me his part yet. "What about you, little man? You from that village, too? "

Rafiq shook his head. "Next village over. Very close. We traded with Abas and Delara's village. A month after their village had their night of terror, the manzazu and his followers showed up at my village. They made demands; food, supplies, young women, and infants. When our elders balked, the manzazu promised to bring the same curse on the village as he had our neighbors. The elders knew that they were powerless, so they gave in.

"The manzazu sent his men to each village in the area, each month, to collect his bounty. That was before we were even born."

Abas resumed, when Rafiq fell silent. He cleared his throat gruffly, shook his head, and spat into a cup. "We moved to this country, my parents and I, after your soldiers came to Afghanistan. We didn't believe that your soldiers could defeat the evil, but perhaps your coming could provide for us a means of escape.

"My parents purchased this ambulance service, believing that we were finally in control of our own future, and could build a better life. Then *he* appeared, a nightmare from the past, and demanded our subservience, again!" Abas finished with a growl, slamming his fist into his thigh in anger.

I looked at him. "But how? I mean, why? What does he demand of you now, in this country?"

Abas raised his head. His dark eyes burned into mine. "He demands raw materials, Marine. We pick up bodies. They get taken to one specific funeral home, where he works his arcane magic to build his army. He has several strongholds, but our part of his operation is just with the funeral home. We know that he has more because he has bragged about it; threatened us that if we do not fulfill our obligation, he will send his undead from another place to kill us."

"We believe him," Rafiq whispered, staring at the floor. The receptionist shuddered, and withdrew into herself even further, if that was possible.

"Well, you won't have to worry for very long, I'm going to shut him down. Permanently," I announced, in what I hoped was a firm, trustworthy tone. "Believe me, now. This shit is going to end.

"So, tell me the name of the funeral home. And the address. I will take care of this," I said, standing up in one smooth motion. Maybe they'd be reassured by my size and coordination.

The three looked at each other. As one, their heads turned toward me. The same expression of disbelief was on each face. It seemed that my size and obvious coordination wasn't very reassuring.

"C'mon, what have you got to lose? Just give me the name of the funeral home. There is no way the guy could know it came from you."

Abas stood, too. "I will tell you, but you are wrong. He can find out, and most likely, he will. And he will likely have his revenge on me. But I am tired of living like this. It is time to stand up to this monster."

Rafiq grabbed his arm. "Don't. It isn't worth the risk, Abas. And it isn't just you that he will take out his anger on; and not just me. You must think of Delara, as well. Because *he* will."

The receptionist looked up at them. There were tears in her eyes. "I don't care. Abas is right. This man," she waved a hand in my direction, "he is right. It is time to end this. I refuse to let this nightmare extend to my children, and their children. It ends now."

She turned to face me directly. "You will end this horror? Or more likely, die trying? I want your word that you will do what you pledge or perish in the attempt."

I just stared back. How many times do I have to repeat myself, my eyes told her. Do I look like someone that doesn't commit fully to the task at hand? I am a Force Recon Marine. Or was.

Abas must have seen the resolve. He stepped closer, and rasped, "Petersen Funeral Home. Just off of Grant at the edge of town. It is on a dark, wooded lot, away from homes and other businesses, perfect for the manzazu's purposes. I trust that you can find your way there," he finished, turning away. "Now go. We have risked enough. Do not speak to us again."

There was nothing clever to say after that, so I simply walked out the back, got back into my truck, and drove back to base; also known as my hotel. I wanted to go straight to the funeral home and kick in the door immediately; it's who and what I am, but I knew that I needed more in the way of firepower first, and some semblance of a plan.

Once back in my wonderful cut-rate hotel room, I loaded up extra magazines with ammo, readied my DPMS, complete with extra mags, and lined up the Glock 19 on the floor next to the rest of the arsenal. Then I sat down at my kitchenette table and used Google Maps to find Petersen Funeral Home. Wonderful thing, Google Maps.

I made four peanut butter sandwiches, and washed them down with a Dr. Pepper. Maybe I was more worn out than I expected, still recovering from my injury, or maybe the food put me into a coma, but for whatever reason, I put my head down on my arms at the table and dozed off.

CHAPTER 21

"Jesus Christ!" I yelled, bolting upright from the chair, my arms sweeping up protectively in front of me. I looked around in a total panic. There was no one there; I was back in my hotel room, NOT in a destroyed building in Afghanistan. My team was not lying at my feet, freshly killed by the zombies. The undead were not coming for me. At least, they weren't in the room with me. Yet.

I stood still, trembling, sweat dripping from my brow. The nightmares were getting worse, and more frequent. Somehow, I had assumed that once I was "all in" on wiping them out, the dreams would go away. It wasn't working.

After checking that the door was still securely locked, and that there wasn't anything lurking in the corners, under the bed, or in the closet, I took a shower. A long one.

It was late, and darkness had fallen. It would probably be best to wait until morning to check out the funeral home, but after my nightmare, staying cooped up in the hotel room was impossible. I needed to do something; go somewhere. Besides, I wasn't going to die a coward. Screw that.

And so, I found myself in my appropriated truck, weapons bag beside me on the seat, driving out to Petersen Funeral Home, trying my best to feel in control and invincible. It wasn't working.

Invincible? You? Bates snorted. *In control? Boy, you ain't even in control of your own damn bowel movements.*

I gritted my teeth and lowered my head. And kept driving. I found Grant Street and followed it to the outskirts of town. My pulse was racing, and my hands were sweaty on the wheel, but I was not going to stop. "I am too invincible. I am an unstoppable killing machine; a lean, mean, fighting machine. I am fucking invincible," I told myself. "Go to hell, Bates."

Whatever my old drill instructor was going to say was interrupted by the phone. The robotic but still identifiable as female voice announced, "In five hundred feet, your destination is on the right."

I looked right and saw only trees. "You have arrived," Google Maps informed me. I slowed, still not seeing a sign. A narrow lane cut between two of the trees, barely visible in the headlights of my old truck. I cranked the wheel, almost missing the turn.

The truck swung onto the lane, headlights flashing onto a dark building a hundred yards ahead. A sign stood unlit next to the building, briefly illuminated by my lights. Sure enough, Petersen Funeral Home. Never doubt the Google, I told myself.

Nice going, asshole, Bates growled. *Subtle. If there IS anyone there, they sure as hell know that you're here. Why not just walk up and ring the bell?*

He was right. Pulling in with my lights on had cost me any chance at a covert entry. Oh well, I'd already used my covert card for the day. Sneaking in the back of the ambulance service was pretty clever. This may call for a more direct approach.

So I did just what Bates said; I pulled up to the front door, parked the truck, and rang the damn bell. I could hear it echo inside. I didn't hear any movement. I waited.

Apparently no one was coming to answer the door. Cowards. I started to feel better. Marines were designed to move forward, to act; not to sit, not to react.

You mean not to think, Corporal? Lt. Ramirez asked, somewhat sarcastically.

Why are all the voices in my head assholes? Why isn't my third-grade teacher offering me advice? Mrs. Black had been nice. She had believed in me; thought I could grow up and make something of myself. Her voice would have been welcome.

I rang the bell again. There were still no sounds of activity from within. I pounded on the door; nothing. I shook my head. I hadn't driven all the way out here for nothing. I pondered for a moment. If I hadn't been able to see the mortuary from the road, then neither could anyone else.

Which meant that I could explore. I hoped there wasn't an alarm system. My tech skills were nonexistent. My version of subtle entry was to put my elbow through the glass viewing port on the door, reach inside and twist the deadbolt, and shove the door open.

My version of subtle worked on this door just fine. The door swung wide, and no alarm sounds split the night air. I thought about grabbing my AR-15 from the weapons bag on the front seat of the truck but decided that it'd be easier to explore with just the handgun and a flashlight.

I drew my Para and stepped inside. A quick look around the door frame and nearby walls revealed no sign of an alarm system, and I heard nothing. I didn't feel anything, either. The place felt empty. Or dead.

With that pleasant thought in my head, I pulled out my Streamlight and turned it on. The tiny flashlight was brighter than most large Maglites, and I never went anywhere without it.

The foyer that I was standing in was standard fare for a funeral home. Pleasant, understated cheerful, and bland. I'm sure during visiting hours, with the lights on and other people around, it was quite nice. Late at night, dark, with only a flashlight and alone, it was creepy.

I figured that the rest of the place would be worse. Maybe I should just go home...climb into bed, pull the covers over my head, and wait for daylight. And maybe I should just join the Girl Scouts, I snorted. This was just another recon mission. I could handle this.

I crept out into the main hallway, light aimed low. If at all possible, I wanted to be able to see without sending too much light out of the windows. Covert. Sneaky. Less likely to get caught and/or mauled by zombies.

The first three rooms that I checked were also standard fare; two of them were smaller "viewing" rooms, the other was a chapel, for services. Nothing out of the ordinary. I ignored the bathrooms, thinking that there would be nothing to find there.

Working to the back, I came upon the receiving area. This large room unlocked from the inside, which made my entrance much easier. It also probably meant that there wouldn't be anything to find here, either. So far, my big tip was a big zilch.

I stood in the middle of the room, shining my light around in an attempt to find something, anything, out of the ordinary. Grumpy, I kicked a gurney. It rolled to the wall and smacked hard.

It binged. The wall did, anyway. A button lit up on the wall where the gurney had struck. I could make out an arrow pointing down on the now brightly glowing button. Hot damn! An elevator.

If there was an elevator, there had to be stairs. There was no way I was going to get on an elevator in the middle of the night in a creepy mortuary frequented by the undead. Nuh-uh.

Five minutes later, I found the damn stairs, behind a mostly barricaded and covered old wooden door. The stairwell was pitch black and foreboding. Even my Streamlight wonder flashlight could barely cut the darkness. There was a bad smell coming up from the basement, too. Swell.

I clicked the safety off of the Para, glanced heavenward for help, and stepped into the stairwell. I ducked my head reflexively to avoid the inevitable cobwebs, but there weren't any. The stairwell may have looked ancient and unused, but the area was clear of cobwebs. So much for the old movies.

My eyes narrowed as the obvious occurred to me: if there were no cobwebs, it might just be because the stairs were being used, recently and regularly. So just maybe I was on the right track. That made me feel smarter, but it also made me feel a lot more nervous. The light may have trembled just the tiniest bit as I went down the rickety old stairs.

At the bottom, I came up against a locked door. It was an old-fashioned job, with what looked to be a skeleton key opening beneath the knob. I didn't have a skeleton key. What I did have was a size thirteen boot, and 250 pounds of weight behind it.

I took a deep breath, lifted my foot, and lashed out. The old door came clean off of its hinges, and crashed into the darkened room beyond. I have a way of making an entrance. Moving in quickly behind the falling door, I swept the room from left to right with both the flashlight and the handgun.

Empty. The room was large, and had tables and gurneys scattered around, but there were no bad guys waiting for me, living or dead. Or undead. I frowned. It felt anticlimactic. There should have been bad guys.

I looked for a light switch. None. That made no sense, either. There had to be light down here in this stupid empty room. There was a light bulb stuck in a cruddy old socket, hanging from the ceiling, but no switch on any wall.

Carefully, I stuck the Streamlight between my teeth and reached up with my left hand. The bulb was loose, so I twisted it. Once snugged in, it came on. Wow. This basement was *old*.

There was a loud scraping noise behind one of the walls. I spun, gun locked solid in both hands, safety off. "C'mon, damn it, show yourself," I growled, words garbled by the flashlight stuck between my teeth.

I noticed that the particular wall that the noise had come from wasn't very solid looking. I noticed that it was all paneling, and the other three walls were painted over cement blocks. Genius that I am, I deduced that the wall in front of me was false.

The noise didn't repeat, but it didn't need to. I knew that there was something back there. I grabbed a corner and pulled. Hard. The entire wall section swung open. Apparently, I had picked the right side to pull on; the other side was hinged.

Beyond was another room. The bare bulb didn't reach this far, and I squinted into the gloom. I heard more noises. The Para swept up, and I aimed the Streamlight in the direction of the scrabbling sounds.

There was a freaking corpse sitting in the corner. I was going to shoot it, almost did, but stopped myself when I noticed that it wasn't moving, and its eye sockets remained dim. Next to the dead guy, though, was a rat. It was gnawing on the corpse's arm.

Shuddering, I turned away. I expected to find corpses in a morgue. I didn't expect to find them sitting up, leaned into a corner of a dungeon, with rats eating them. I thought about shooting the rat.

I decided not to, but something from that corner scene bothered me. I turned back and looked closer. There was a garbage can next to the corpse, and there was movement inside the can. Holding the light up high, and keeping the Para trained on the can, I edged closer.

The movement was more rats. They were swarming over what looked like baby dolls. I kicked the can, and rats ran over the rim and scattered. I stared over the rim. My blood curdled as I realized that inside the can was a tangled pile of dead infants. They weren't dolls or toys. They were desiccated dead babies.

As I stood there looking stupid, I heard more noises. They weren't rustling sounds; I heard the elevator moving. That wasn't from rats. I forced myself to leave the horror of the infants and looked around for somewhere to hide. Whoever was coming was probably not expecting to have company.

There wasn't anywhere to hide my 6'5" frame in this musty old basement. I heard the elevator settle with a thud, and the doors started to open. Desperate, I ducked behind the paneling wall and pulled it closed. I wouldn't be able to see out, but any port in a storm.

I heard the doors open, and several dragging, scraping footsteps.

The doors closed. There were no voices, and the only breathing I could hear was my own. I was getting a really bad feeling.

From behind me, I heard the rat squeak and scrabble. I didn't let it distract me. The action was on the other side of the paneling. Single minded focus was an attribute of the hard charging Marine, and I was representative of that particular species.

As I was congratulating myself on being so purposeful, a cold hand grabbed me by the back of my neck. I screamed in surprise and outrage, jumping out of my skin.

My shout must have been the signal for whatever ambush I'd just let myself get suckered into, because the paneling immediately swung open, pulled from the other side with great violence. Swell. So much for single minded focus.

My attention was now divided; something had a hold of me from the rear, and several somethings were coming at me from the front. I couldn't afford to look away from the room in front of me; I just knew that bad creepy things were going to materialize, now that the wall had been shoved aside.

On the other hand, I already knew what was attacking me from behind, and I didn't want it to bite me any more than I wanted the things in front of me to. So I did what I do best: I stopped thinking, and let my body take over.

A quick sidestep right, combined with a twisting upward swimming motion with my left arm freed me from the thing behind me, and allowed me to keep the Para pointed out into the main room. Which was good, since there were four pairs of red eyes glaring at me, closing fast.

I blasted all four pairs, twice each. In theory, double taps are most useful with a 9mm handgun, like a Sig P226, the old Navy Seal standby, and not considered necessary for a heavy .45 like my 1911, but I was freaked out and not totally rational. Flight or fight response had kicked in, and the "fight" part was in full swing.

No sooner had the seventh and eighth shots rang out, then I stepped forward and pivoted to the rear, putting three rounds into the shambling corpse that had grabbed me from behind. Its head basically disintegrated, and it flopped to the ground.

I spun back to the front, sensing movement. There was no way I could have heard anything or anyone moving; eleven full power .45 ACP rounds going off in enclosed confines had my ears ringing in a most painful manner.

Blinking through the smoke, I felt rather than heard someone on the stairs, moving away. I pushed forward, kicking my way through the various corpses scattered on the floor. My adrenaline was pumping through my veins; I had just taken out five more of my supernatural enemy; I was *jacked*.

I hit the stairs at full speed, no thought of caution or safety in my head. Whatever was attempting to flee had no chance.

Except that it did. Whatever it was, it was faster than I was. I wasn't half way up the staircase when I heard the door slam. The good news was my hearing was coming back. The bad news was that my unseen assailant was gone. By the time I made it outside, the taillights of whatever vehicle had brought in my ambushers was just vanishing from sight. Damn.

I walked around the funeral home back to my truck. I was disappointed and angry at myself, but I wasn't distracted enough to not pay extra close attention to my surroundings; I'd just been ambushed once, and no one said that you couldn't be ambushed twice.

The interior light went on as I opened the driver's side door to the old Ford. The moment the light went on I realized that I was vulnerable, and at that same moment a hole appeared in the seat. A fraction of a second later, I heard the sharp crack of the would-be assassin's rifle.

Not bothering to close the door, I turned and dove to the ground, rolling. There was another crack, and grass and dirt flew into the air, inches from where my head was. It was hard to be sure with the chaos of everything going on, but I thought that the second shot came from a different direction than the first one had.

I rolled to my feet and then leaped in a different direction, hitting and rolling back up, snatching the Para from its holster and trying to find a target. There was a tree to my left that could hide someone, and I saw moonlight glint off a scope at the end of the building to my right.

There was no chance of taking out either target from where I was, and I was too exposed anyway. I took two quick steps toward the truck and then zagged toward the building. Both shooters fired, putting their shots ahead of where I had been going.

I gained the front door before they could adjust and ducked inside. I sprinted to the end of the building in the dark, trusting in my memory of the layout. If the pair outside did things by the book, the one behind the tree would cover the one at the end of the building. That guy would come to the door first, and then cover the guy at the tree while he closed in.

So I went out the side door at the end of the building, and ended up behind the guy coming to the door. I stepped around the corner and shot the guy in the back of the head, and ducked back before his cover could swing around and shoot me.

Once back inside, I slipped back down the hallway, past the front door, and halfway to the other end of the building. I found a window that faced out at the driveway, and eased it far enough up to shoot my pistol out from.

I waited. Either the guy behind the tree would come in, or he'd leave. I figured that he'd been left with his partner by the manzazu with an order to kill me, so he'd stay to finish his job. The necromancer probably wasn't a very forgiving sort.

There was a possibility of police showing up because of the gunfire, but that didn't concern me too much. If anything, cops would be a bigger issue for the other shooter than it was for me. The guy would have to make his move soon.

He did. Cautiously, a dark shape moved from behind the tree and came toward the funeral home. Whoever the guy was, he moved well but not like a trained pro. A real pro would have crawled in from that spot and not given an enemy a decent side shot from the window that I was currently crouched at.

I let him get close. At twenty yards he could see that the window was halfway up to his right. He froze in place, looking hard in my direction. The moonlight outlined his form while not giving anything away at my location, inside the building.

He swung his rifle toward window, either to shoot at me or simply to try and look through his scope at the open window. Either way, it was time. I shot twice, hitting him once in the chest. He staggered and then dropped and didn't move again.

I went outside and checked both men. They were of middle-eastern descent. Each one had an AR-15 and a Glock handgun. Each of them was dead. Neither had any ID on them.

Time to go home and regroup. The funeral home was a bust. It had been a setup from the beginning. Clearly my new "allies" weren't as honest and helpful as I thought. Maybe I should revisit them. Obviously, they weren't as afraid of me as they were the manzazu.

They chose the wrong team. I was going to have to explain that to them. Right after I placed an anonymous call to the police and told them about the murdered infants at the funeral home.

CHAPTER 22

"You set me up!" I growled, slamming Rafiq up against wall. Both of my fists were wrapped up in his shirt, which would have left me vulnerable to his partner, if he'd been inclined to step in. Which he wasn't. It didn't matter to me. Right now I welcomed the risk. A good ass kicking would have helped my mood immensely.

It had taken me all day to find these turkeys, and my frustration levels had built, climbing higher and higher into the red zone as each place I'd looked had come up dry. The office had been closed; the lady dispatcher was nowhere to be found. So I'd driven around all day, hoping to find the right ambulance by random chance. It wasn't a great plan, and had taken nine hours to work.

"Why?" I demanded, shaking the little man. "Are you that in love with what this monster is doing? Are you part of this?"

Rafiq twisted in my grip, trying to free himself. I pushed him back against the wall again, and drove him upward, sliding up the rough brick until his feet left the ground. "I oughta just kill you. Maybe your boss will make you into one of his pets."

The other guy moved closer, raising his hands. "Don't even think about it, asshole," I snapped over my shoulder. "You're next, Abas.

My guess is that you're both working for the manzazu; your lady friend probably is, too."

"Stop. We didn't set you up. We're not working for anyone but ourselves," Abas said, grabbing one of my arms and trying to tug it away from Rafiq. I snorted. The twerp had about as much chance of prying my arm away as I did of winning the lottery. In England.

"Keep it up; you're gonna get his neck snapped. I only need one of you," I told Abas. "And I don't care which of you it is." I turned my attention back to the squirming Rafiq. "Now, tell my why you set me up. And how."

The EMT seemed to realize at last that I was serious and settled down. He stopped struggling, and went limp in my grip. I wasn't taking any chances, though, and kept him off the ground, pinned against the wall.

"Well?"

"We aren't working with the manzazu. But he holds our lives in his hands, along with our families. We don't think you can win. It is better to survive. His evil is eternal; your anger is not. We made a choice," he muttered.

"You made a choice to feed me to his freaking zombies? What kind of man does that?" I yelled. We were in a neighborhood where people kept to themselves, but if I kept this up, we'd attract attention. So I tried to dial it down a little.

"I'm the only friend you've got here, and you stabbed me in the back," I whispered, aware of the irony. Last week, I actually *had* been stabbed in the back. By someone else that I'd tried to help. Maybe I should take the hint. I shook him again, fed up with the situation.

"You are not my friend," Rafiq said, making eye contact with me for the first time. "You may think that you are, but you are not. He is," Rafiq nodded over my shoulder at Abas. "We must think of ourselves and our families. If you truly understood anything, you would know this. The manzazu has decreed that you and your Colonel must die. It is regrettable, but there is nothing that anyone can do about it. Beating me up will not change anything."

I dropped him in shock. "What the hell did you just say?"

Rafiq looked away. "I said nothing can change destiny. The manzazu is going to kill you. I just want to be left alone," he said.

I frowned. "Not that. What you said about 'your Colonel must die.' What the hell do you mean by that?" I slammed a hand on the wall on either side of him, so that he couldn't get away. He kept his eyes averted.

Abas intervened. "He simply meant that the manzazu will have his revenge, on anyone who gets in his way. It has been that way for generations, and will be so in the future as well. It is fate; karma."

I spun to glare at him. "No. He said 'your Colonel.' Not 'anyone.' My Colonel. I want to know what he meant by that. How do you even know who my Colonel is? Or, was," I amended. I am not a Marine anymore. Just a pissed off civilian. A very pissed off civilian.

Both men looked at each other and then away. Rafiq mumbled something that I couldn't quite catch. Abas replied to him, speaking quickly in their native tongue. I didn't understand a single rapid fire word, and I really disliked being excluded from the conversation.

So I shot one hand out and caught Abas by the throat and slammed him up against the wall next to his friend. I didn't have the leverage to push both of them up off of the ground one-handed, but I could and did pin them hard up against the brick.

"Now get this straight, assholes," I growled quietly. "I spent two tours over in your shitbox country, and I put down more of your kind than I can count. I came home and just wanted to be left alone. Your manzazu came after me, and you know that he's after Colonel LeMasters, too. So I want him. I'm going to put him down, and if I have to, I have no compunction against putting you rats in the ground next to him."

"I'm going to ask you straight up questions, and you're going to give me straight answers, and then I'm going to leave you. If you don't answer, you won't be breathing when I leave. Got it?" I asked, leaning in even farther.

To my surprise, the men got angry. They stiffened, and glared at me. I thought that I was going to have to kill them, and I didn't know if I actually could, despite my threats. I'd never killed anything or anyone who wasn't trying to kill me.

Rafiq grabbed my wrist with both hands. He didn't try to pull free; he just pushed back against my grip on his throat so that he could speak. "You are so American. Such a Rambo. You think that blundering about, shoving and shouting will accomplish that you want.

"This sorcerer has existed for centuries. Your mind can not even grasp what his life is; how powerful he is, and how deep his tentacles reach. You have no chance, and your Colonel is doomed as well. It is possible, that if the manzazu chooses, America itself may fall under his sway," Rafiq spat. "You are just a temporary inconvenience to him."

Abas piled on. "We would resist if we could. He holds our families here captive, and has the power to destroy our entire family lines back home as well. How do you think he arrived safely in this country of yours? Do you think that Delara wanted to hide him here, after all he has done? She had no choice, just as we don't."

My eyes narrowed. "What do you mean, 'Delara wanted to hide him here?' Is he with her?"

Both men shook their heads. "No," they both said. I tightened my grip.

"Talk to me," I demanded.

Abas croaked, "The manzazu forced Delara to hide him when he arrived in this country. She had no choice," he added.

I relaxed my grip enough that he could talk normally.

"He threatened her child, Marine. You cannot understand what that means, but she had no choice but to give him a place to stay," he said.

"So where is this place? Tell me where Delara lives," I growled.

"He is no longer there," Rafiq said.

I snickered. "You'll forgive me if I don't take you at your word. Tell me where she lives. Or take me there."

Rafiq glared at me. "He is not there, Marine. He left three weeks ago, and when he did, he took her child, to ensure her cooperation. And ours. We do not know where he is. If we did, we would know where the child is."

"We do not even know where Delara is. She did not come in to work today, and she is not home. We were there. Going back to her house is a waste of time," Aziz added.

"You already lied to me once, and set me up. If you do it again, you're toast," I threatened them.

They looked confused at the last comment. I guess that threat didn't translate very well. I tried again. "Tell me where to find this piece of shit. Now."

Abas grimaced. "We don't know. He has been consolidating his power, building an army. Recently, he moved his base of operations out of that funeral home. I don't know where they went. We were just instructed to send you there."

It was Rafiq's turn. "We know that his immediate plans were to eliminate the Colonel, in return for the Colonel's role in destroying his stronghold in Afghanistan. Have you seen the Colonel recently, Marine?"

His question caught me off guard. I considered. In truth, I hadn't seen him for several days, when we were both at the shrink's office. It was looking like I needed to check on him. Immediately.

I dropped Rafiq and Abas. "I don't suppose either of you know where the Colonel lives, do you?"

They both looked at me incredulously. Like I'd lost my mind. As I thought about it, it occurred to me that perhaps I had. I glared as I heard sarcastic laughter somewhere in the back of my brain. Bates, no doubt.

"Never mind," I told them. "I'll find him myself. How hard can it be?"

"We commend your bravery, Marine, but it will avail you nothing. You would be better served to flee. Move west, far from here. The manzazu will still find you, but it will take longer," Abas told me.

I snorted. "Hasn't worked for him so far, has it? I think I'm up about fifty dead zombies to zero on him."

"You understand nothing. You are playing checkers with a being that is playing chess," Rafiq said. He shook his head sadly. "It is unfortunate; you have many fine qualities. It would have been an honor to have you as a friend in this, our new country."

Abas took Rafiq's arm and led him away from me, toward their ambulance. Hastily, they climbed in and drove off. It was almost like they wanted to get as far away from me as possible, as fast as possible.

I stood in place, staring like an idiot after the disappearing ambulance. My threats and promises had made no impression on them. They were either evil themselves, which I doubted, or they were just that scared of the necromancer and that resigned to the outcome of my mission.

Shaking my head, I turned back to my old battered truck. I still had a job to do. By their account, there was an assassination plot aimed at my old commander. My enemy had been stockpiling his weapons of war.

I needed to get to the Colonel as fast as possible. The manzazu had been ramping up his attempts on me; it only made sense that he'd do the same with LeMasters. The VA wasn't too far away. I'd go there first and see if he was still at work. If he wasn't, I'd get his address and go there.

It wasn't the most complicated of plans, but I was taught the KISS Principle: "Keep It Simple, Stupid." Who could argue with KISS? I started the truck, put it in gear, and took off for my first stop: the VA Hospital.

Just in case he was gone, and his secretary wasn't obliged to give me his address, I'd have to get it from Sovers. He had to know LeMasters' address. It wouldn't be public knowledge; I knew that much. It would be private; protected; like a cop's home address. But Sovers had a Rolodex on his desk, and I'd bet my Para that an important guy like the Colonel would be in it. On second thought, I'd bet my Glock

19 on it. The Para was too important to wager on my faulty reasoning.

Traffic was with me, and I rolled into the VA parking lot in just fifteen minutes. I really needed to get into the various offices and floors quickly, so I did the unthinkable and unpacked all of my weapons and locked them in the glovebox.

I stepped out of the truck and froze. I felt absolutely naked. Speed was good; speed AND a way to defend myself was better. Reached back into the truck and pulled a newer toy from under the seat. Smiling grimly, I tucked the Cold Steel carbon fiber knife into my right sock.

Shaking my pants leg back down over my boot, I checked my six. Clear. Feeling much better about life, I hustled across the parking lot and in through the front door of the hospital. I made my way to the administrative offices and walked up to LeMasters' secretary. That particularly efficient example of government worker looked up at me, glanced at the clock on the wall, and sighed.

"Yes?" She asked, resigned to my intrusion.

I knew that her day ended in fifteen minutes, but I was willing to risk her unhappiness. "Please, ma'am, is the Colonel in? I really need to see him," I asked her, honey dripping from my voice.

"The Colonel is not in his office, sir. I'm sorry. Perhaps you can try again tomorrow," she replied, looking relieved that I wouldn't be keeping her late after all.

"Are you sure? It's important," I said.

She pursed her lips in annoyance. "Of course I'm sure. He hasn't been in all day. Now, if there's nothing else, I have some things to do before going home. Have a nice day," she said by way of dismissal.

"Can you give me the Colonel's address? I need to see him," I asked, knowing as I said it that it wouldn't work.

"That's private information, sir. Sorry. Now, as I said..." she trailed off, looking pointedly at the clock on the wall.

"Yeah. Fine. Thanks a bunch," I grumbled and left with poor

grace. I had just enough time to get up and over to psych on the fifth floor and try my luck with Sovers.

I trooped up the stairs, trying to be more quiet than normal. My size thirteen combat boots made entirely too much noise in the cavernous stairwell. If there were people (or things!) lying in wait for me, they'd know I was coming for sure. I reached the fifth floor landing unmolested.

Reaching down, I patted the knife to make sure it was still there. Truth time. Cold Steel marketed their carbon fiber knives with the claim that they were invisible to metal detectors. We're about to find out, I told myself, and opened the door to the psych ward reception room.

The same disapproving look from the receptionist greeted my entrance. Actually, she added a frown. Nice. She had range. Like Kristen Stewart.

"Mr. Brooks, what are you doing here? Your next appointment with Doctor Sovers isn't until tomorrow afternoon," she informed me coldly. Having spoken, she turned her face away from me. I was dismissed.

I walked up to her desk and planted my hands solidly on either side of her monitor. Leaning over her, I growled, "I need to see the doc. Now."

She wasn't impressed. She'd dealt with a lot of deranged ex-soldiers, apparently. I wasn't going to intimidate her. Time to switch tactics.

Sovers and the other doctors had decided early on in my treatment that I shouldn't stay in the waiting room with other patients. I was unsettling. So, I took my hands off of the receptionist's desk and smiled. I tried to make it as sickly as possible.

"That's okay. I understand. These other nice people were here first. I can't just cut in line," I announced, waving my arm to indicate the half dozen patients watching me closely. "I'll just wait here and take my turn. Probably be good to socialize, anyway."

With a heavy sigh, I collapsed into a chair next to an old man with a scrawny neck about as big around as my wrist. I shifted as close as I could get to him and smiled my sickly smile again. He recoiled from me, his eyes wide.

"Hey," I stage whispered to him. "Hey, what are you in for? I mean, I know we're all nuts, but what did you do to get sent here? D'ya know what I did?" I asked. I looked around like I was making sure we were all alone. "I killed some people. It's what soldiers do, right? But these people that I killed...they were already dead. How's that for crazy?"

The old guy's eyes almost bugged out of his head. Poor guy. I felt bad, but the mission came first. I put my hand on his arm and he cringed, trying unsuccessfully to pull it away from me.

"They always seem to come out at night. That's why I'm here *now*, so they can't get me. I'm safe while the sun's out," I told him. It wasn't technically true, but he didn't know that. Besides, I was playing to the house.

The severe looking receptionist was looking at me like she'd just bitten into something distasteful. She tapped her earpiece and spoke rapidly. After several seconds, she got up out of her chair and hustled over to me.

"Mr. Brooks, you're in luck. Dr. Sovers had a last second cancellation, and he can see you right now. So let's go in, shall we? Let go of Mr. Dawkins, here; he's fine right where he is. Come right this way," she said, taking me by the arm and trying to drag me to the door.

I let myself be led. "Oh, that's wonderful. I mean, I hope whoever canceled is okay and all, but it really is important that I see my doctor. Thanks, Miss...?" I trailed off, waiting for her to fill in her name.

Apparently, she didn't want me to know her name. She just shook her head and practically threw me through the door into the psych wing. It was okay that I didn't get her name; it wasn't like I was going to ask her out on a date.

I stumbled through the doorway and bumped into Paxton. My favorite security guard. I smiled at him, too. "Hi, buddy. Miss me?"

"Brooks. Great. What the hell are you doing here? I thought you weren't supposed to be here until tomorrow," he grumped, smoothing his shirt. "You should be more careful. You might get hurt, barging in like that."

I gave him a smirk this time. One that told him that he was much more likely to get hurt than I was, and we both knew it. I held my arms out wide, inviting him to search me. He scowled and pointed me to the scanner.

Obviously, Paxton was expecting the alarm to go off. It had last time, and that was after he'd searched me. He even opened the drawer in his desk where he stored my various toys when I came to visit.

"Hey, is my little Sig in there? I never got it back after I got stabbed," I asked and peered in. He kicked the drawer shut and stepped in front of the desk and folded his arms. I resisted the urge to kick him over his desk.

Grumbling inside, I stepped over to the metal detector, took a deep breath, and walked through. I was just sure that the Cold Steel knife would set off the alarm. Paxton watched critically, also certain that I'd set the alarm off.

Nothing happened. The metal detector stayed quiet. Paxton's eyes narrowed. "What the hell? This thing must be broken. You never show up without at least three different weapons that you're not supposed to have."

My innocent angelic expression did nothing to reassure him. He grabbed a wand and motioned at me to stay still while he went over me in minute detail. I was getting bored with this game. I pushed his arm away.

"Stay away from with that thing, asshole. I need to see the doc, and you're being a pain. I passed the freaking metal detector test; now let me go."

He squinted at me. I think it was supposed to be his tough look, but all it really did was make him look like an upright pig. I thought about pointing that out and decided that it wouldn't help matters.

"Brooks, you're up to something. I know it; you know it; the doc knows it. I should keep you out here, but I'm sick of looking at you. Go the hell away," he grumped, waving me down the hallway.

I took "yes" for an answer and double-timed it down to Sovers' door. Without knocking I opened the door and stepped in. Paxton had screwed up. He'd sent me down before the doc told him to. He was still with a patient.

"Oops," I said, trying my best to look embarrassed. "I didn't mean to interrupt. I can wait. Go ahead and finish," I offered. "I'll just sit here," I said and sat in a chair set in the corner of the office.

The patient, who didn't look much older than I was, turned his startled gaze to the doctor. Sovers, ever the smug son of a bitch, nodded thoughtfully, like he was considering my offer. After waiting long enough to let the tension build, he put down his notebook and looked up.

"No, Jeffrey, I think we're done today. You're doing fine; I'm very encouraged. I think we can afford to wrap things up a little early this time, don't you? I will see you next week at this same time," he said, standing up to usher the young vet up and out of the room.

The guy stood, still looking confused. He turned to look at me again, and resentment began to show on his face. His lip curled, and he started to make a snide comment. I kept my hands at my sides, but my eyes must have shown something because he flinched and backed down.

Without a word, the young man left. He did remind me that I was not his favorite, by slamming the door as hard he could. It wasn't very impressive. I ignored it and remained standing, sort of at attention, but mostly just trying to get a covert look at Sovers' desk. I needed that Rolodex.

"Well, Mr. Brooks, you insisted on this meeting. What can I do for you today? Are you healing up from your last unfortunate incident?" Sovers asked, seating himself behind his desk. Apparently this session wasn't going to be the friendly type where we sit facing each in his overstuffed easy chairs. All brisk and business today.

I sat in the chair in front of his desk, forcing myself to adopt a casual posture. I even slouched. "I just really need to talk, doc."

"About what, Chase?" Sovers asked, all polite interest. He used my first name again, which made me bristle. Which the bastard noticed. I know, because he smiled faintly.

Careful Marine, I heard Lt. Rodriquez warn. *Remember the mission. Don't get sidetracked on shit that doesn't matter.* I took a deep breath and held it.

"Doc, those things that I saw are real. I tried to pretend that they were just in my imagination, but they're real. I need to know what to do about them," I blurted out. It wasn't my intention to tell the truth; I really didn't want to get locked up.

The good doctor blinked. He stared at me for a good thirty seconds. Finally, he said, "Mr. Brooks, that is a serious problem. I thought that we were past this point. This is concerning."

"It's not that big a deal, doc. It's not like I ever believed that they were in my imagination anyway. I always knew that they were real. I'm just coming clean about it. By the way, do you happen to know where Colonel LeMasters is?" I asked. I'm subtle.

"It IS a big deal, Mr. Brooks. One that we'll have to deal with, and quickly. As for the Colonel," he paused. "The Colonel has better things to do than be constantly bothered by one ex-Marine with authority issues, and obvious issues with reality."

He picked up a notebook and began thumbing through it. "Yes, here we go," he mumbled. "I think that we need some thorough testing, Mr. Brooks, as soon as possible. Let me see," the good doctor said, picking up his phone. "Let me call and see how soon we can get you in. You'll need the standard cognitive battery, and the basic aggression quotient, and..." he trailed off, considering.

"On second thought, I should go in person and ensure that we get all the tests that you need, Chase," he stated, replacing the phone in its cradle and rising to his feet. Inside, I smiled hugely. Being left alone with his Rolodex was the entire reason that I was here.

"Let me just call Corporal Paxton to come down and sit with you while I'm gone," Sovers announced, picking his phone back up, and causing my heart to plummet. *So much for being smooth and cool,* I could hear my old patrol mate McGavin chide.

Desperately, I waved him off. I stood up, my brain racing to find an answer. Inspiration struck. I smiled ruefully and patted my leg. "You know, that's a great idea. I was naughty, and slipped a carbon fiber fighting blade past him and his metal detector. If he comes down here, it gives me a chance to fess up and give it to him," I informed him, and slipped the knife out of my sock.

"Yeah," I added, studying the edge of the blade critically. "We'll have a great discussion over this, doc. Don't worry about us; we're practically best friends."

Sovers froze. I don't think he was afraid of me with the knife, but he was intelligent enough to know that not only were Paxton and I emphatically not friends, but that we would not handle this situation safely or quietly. I'm sure various scenarios, all bad, played out in his head.

He replaced the phone again, and glared at me. "Mr. Brooks, you are positively the most trying patient that I have. Did you intend to use that knife against me, your doctor and best ally to recovery? Shame on you," he scolded me.

"You just stay right here in my office. I'll be right back," he promised, sliding past me, careful to remain facing me at all times. I'm telling you, the doctor knew combative theory, at the least. He made it to the door and rushed out, trying but not completely keeping his dignity. "And don't get into anything," he threw over his shoulder on his way out.

Take that, asshole, I told McGavin. He had never been the most supportive patrol partner, but he was a good guy to have at my back in a firefight. I was surprised that he was speaking to me now, too. Usually the voices in my head were authority figures.

I outsmarted a shrink, I told them all, *and you think my people skills are lacking? Screw you guys,* I smirked. Sgt. Bates was quick to put me back in my place.

Yeah, good for you, brainiac. Hurry up and find that address. Your doc is not only coming back, intent on locking you up, but because you pulled a knife on him, he won't be coming back alone. Genius, he grumped.

He was right. I grabbed the Rolodex and thumbed through it. Bingo! Colonel James Franklin LeMasters, retired, 2362 Fairview Rd, Chesapeake, VA. Perfect, I told myself. I could find that; Google Maps is a wonderful thing. Now to get out of the hospital without getting myself committed against my will.

I opened the door and peeked out. Sure enough, Sovers was coming down the hall with Paxton and three other guards. Four guys just for me? I was flattered.

Ducking back inside, I placed the carbon fiber blade on the doctor's desk and then sat down in the patient chair. I crossed my ankles and leaned back, looking as innocent and safe as any Recon Marine that stands 6'5" and weighs 250 pounds could look.

The door opened and Paxton poked his head in. He saw me and grimaced. "Oh yeah, Dr. Sovers, he's still here," he announced. Like I could be anywhere else, I thought and rolled my eyes.

The entire group moved cautiously through the doorway. The four Marine guards surrounded me, and Sovers worked his way around to his desk. He looked at me, glanced down at his desk, saw the knife, and looked back at me.

I gave him my best contrite face. "Doc, I've been thinking about it while you were gone, and I don't think I'm ready to talk about things after all. The zombies were just in my head, like you said," I told him, rhyming like a master rapper. He didn't seem impressed.

"What do you mean, Mr. Brooks? You brought a weapon into my office and threatened me with it. Corporal Paxton and his team are here to take you to a solitary room until we can begin your treatment," the doctor informed me, and motioned to the men.

Without any warning, I leapt to my feet. All four guards flinched and much, much too late to do any good had this been a life or death situation, they jumped back. I raised my arms, showing my hands.

"Look, I'm not armed. The knife is on your desk, sir. It was simply an oversight. I always carry a knife; I just forgot that I had it. It isn't my fault that Paxton is too bad at his job to find it. If anything, you should thank me for pointing out this obvious flaw in the search and pat down part of your program. A real Marine wouldn't have missed an eight-inch blade," I said, casting a disapproving look at Paxton. He glared back at me, flexing his hands in anger.

"I need to go, doc. I'll see you tomorrow for my regular appointment. Keep the knife; you can give it back to me tomorrow. See ya," I told Sovers, and sidestepped between the tense guards smoothly. I made it out the door without anyone grabbing me. Apparently they were going to let me out, this time.

Go big or go home, I told myself. "Maybe I can pick up my Sig 938 tomorrow too, doc. I miss that little gun. Since I don't have it, I've started carrying a bigger gun. You don't want that on your conscience, do you?"

Sovers yelled after me, "You're not getting that firearm back, Brooks. Tomorrow you'll be put on a twenty-four-hour psych hold, unless you can bring me absolute proof that your zombie fantasy is true. Do you hear me, Brooks? It's put up or shut up time."

His words echoed in my head all the way down the stairs and back out to my truck. Why in the world had he said that? He didn't believe me, and had spent months trying to get me to admit that they were made up; manifestations of guilt for surviving while my team died. The guy was crazier than he accused me of being.

What an asshat.

CHAPTER 23

I GOT BACK to my room at the fleabag hotel and fired up my computer. I knew that I could just use Google Maps on my phone to find the Colonel's place, but I wanted to plan this out better. "Information is power" my instructors had beaten into my head.

Strangely, I was not as exhilarated as I was tired. I was using my brain much more than my brawn and I wasn't used to fighting that way. It wasn't as rewarding, and it was much harder, to boot.

While the computer was busy coming to life, I grabbed a piece of paper to map out my course of action. I made a list of the weapons that I was going to bring with me, which was all of them, and tried to list other equipment that I'd need. It was impossible. I couldn't know what I'd need in advance; I didn't know what the Colonel's place was like.

Firing my pen at the far wall, I turned to my screen. The stupid computer was finally up and ready. I typed in *James Franklin LeMasters* in the search bar and sat back. After several eons, the screen flashed with results. I found the one that I was looking for and clicked on it.

The Colonel had style, and a fancy palatial estate. It was featured in several magazines and local newspaper stories. My eyes bugged out at some of the pictures. My former commander lived in his own version of Disney World.

"Wow," I breathed. I assumed he'd have security; a gate and high walls. I would never have guessed that he would have his own small town. In addition to the gigantic house, there was a separate four-car garage, a guard house/barracks, and a small guest house. Being a Colonel paid better than being a Corporal. In fairness, I knew that his wife was some wealthy socialite as well.

I retrieved my pen, and started sketching out a plan of attack. After a couple of hours of drawing, scratching out, cursing, and revising, I rubbed my eyes and sat back. I hoped none of my elaborate battle plans would be necessary. I hoped I'd show up at the Colonel's place and he'd be there, all safe and sound, and just let me in. I'd tell him about the manzazu and the connection with Delara, and together we'd take care of business.

Before shutting down the laptop and getting on my way I checked the local news. It never hurt to see what was going on, and I needed to know if there was anything being reported about my activities.

Running first on the news was break in at the Chesapeake Zoo. A Bengal tiger had been stolen. It hadn't escaped, it had been taken. There was video footage of a panel truck going through the closed gates, backing up to the tiger enclosure, and then several hooded figures coaxing a large male tiger up into the back of the truck. The reporter said that police were reviewing the footage, but as of yet there were no leads.

Weird. But it didn't really concern me. The next story did. It was about my escapade from the previous night. There was a story about a break in at the Peterson Funeral Home, where apparently there was a fight amongst the criminals, and two of them had been killed. The rest of the gang was on the loose.

I chuckled. At least they got part of it right; I was very much on the loose. For at least the next twenty hours or so. We'd have to see if Sovers made good on his threat to commit me against my will.

Shutting down the laptop, I turned and grabbed my weapons bag. Time to get down to business, I told myself. I loaded my Para, stuck it in its holster, and stashed three more loaded magazines in mag pouches on my belt. The Glock 19 went into the underarm holster on the left side of my carry shirt. Extra mags for that went on the right side. Various knives and even brass knuckles went into various pockets and sheaths. I started to feel heavy.

Lastly, I went to the closet and grabbed my DPMS AR-15, with its new red dot sight. It felt awkward in my hands, and my brain flashed to that Wilson Combat 458 Socom sitting at Bill's shop. I shook my head, and told the voices to leave me alone. The DPMS would be fine.

I grabbed a PMAG and stuck it into the rifle, making sure it seated clean, and then reached to grab two more off of the shelf. And came to an abrupt halt. They were empty. I only had one loaded magazine for my AR. Those thirty rounds would go fast in a serious firefight. I needed more ammo.

Grumbling, I slid the AR into its bag, zipped it closed, and headed for the door. I needed to stop at Freeman Lock and Alarm and visit the old geezer that ran the place. Normally that was the best part of my week. Now it was an unwanted distraction that I didn't have time for.

Twenty minutes later, I shoved the door open and listened to the bell announce my presence at Freeman's. I heard an old voice grumble, and the sound of something heavy thumping down onto a work bench.

Bill came wandered out, blinking in the bright light of the store. "What the hell do you want?" He demanded, glaring. Then his face cleared, and he smiled. "Never mind. I know. Just a second," he said, waving me to wait where I was.

In a few moments he was back, with a Blackhawk rifle bag. He held it up with a grin. "I have it all ready for you. You've got three nine-round mags; Lancer, they cycle better, and two twenty round boxes of 300 grain Xtreme Penetrator rounds. No sling, but you're a big boy; you can just carry the damn thing," he told me. "Here, check it out," he invited, unzipping the top of the bag.

"Bill, what the hell are you talking about? I'm here to buy four or five boxes of 5.56. That's it. You can keep your high priced toy. You bought it for yourself; I don't need it," I informed him, trying not to look at the rifle nestled inside the case. It was talking to me again, its seductive voice promising me sweet rewards and recoil.

Resolutely, I turned my head away from the Wilson Combat and my expectant shop owner. I pointed off to my right. "That's where you keep the rifle ammo. Just get me five boxes of Winchester X; they'll be fine for what I need."

Bill lowered the soft case. He stared at me for a long time. His right eye twitched. Finally, he cleared his throat. "Boy, you been comin' in here for a long time. You're kinda as close to being my son as anybody. I know you. I don't know what shit you're in, but you need this rifle. Your face was in my head when I placed the order three months ago.

"I set this up for me; put an Eotech on it with a magnifier. It felt wrong. If you look at it now, you'll see I took it off. Put a Holosun red circle reflex sight on it. Its motion activated, so you don't even have to turn it on. You pick it up, it comes on as fast as you can shoulder it. Felt right.

"Those three Lancer mags are designed for this cartridge, and I ordered them special to go with it. I don't need three damn mags for a beast like this. But I think that you do. So don't be an idiot. Take the damn gun," he growled. For a little guy in his seventies, he was pretty formidable. I almost took it.

"No. I don't have the money for a gun like this," I lied. In my mind, I could see the pile of cash sitting in my hotel room. "I just need my ammo, and then I'm off. C'mon, Bill, it's important," I told him, almost begging. Almost. I'm way too tough to actually beg.

His eyes narrowed. "In a hurry, are you? Where's the fire?"

Desperate to change the subject, I told him. "I need to get to my CO. I think he's in trouble."

"Trouble that requires a hundred rounds of 5.56, and you all weighed down with the Para, your damn Glock, and all those blades?" He demanded.

"How the hell do you know what I'm carrying?" I asked defensively. "Who says that I have all that on me?"

He harrumphed. "Boy, I wasn't born yesterday. I can see by how you're carrying yourself what you have on and where. I put the night sights on the Glock, remember? Subtle, you ain't."

"Okay, fine. I'm carrying. Sell me damn ammo and let me get out of here," I grumped back at him. I got places to be."

He shook his head and ambled over the cash register. He rung me up, accepted my cash, and handed me my receipt. "Good luck to you, kid. Come back when this is over, and tell me what happened. Gives me something to look forward to."

I looked away, embarrassed by the emotion in his voice. The old guy actually did care. I nodded. "I'll be back," I told him.

As I went out the door I swear I heard him say, "You better be."

Tough guy that I am, I just kept going.

CHAPTER 24

My drive out to Fairview Road was uneventful. It was a beautiful late afternoon, with sunshine and a light breeze. It was hard to believe that I was on my way to a possible all-out war with a nightmare necromancer and an entire army of the undead.

Nice alliteration, Bates told me. *Don't get distracted by the scenery, asshole. Stay focused. Concentrate on the manzazu.*

He wasn't wrong. According to the EMTs the manzazu had been building an army in preparation for taking out the Colonel. That made the attempts on me just a petty sideline for him. The necromancer was a major weight foe then, and I was going in alone to try and take him out.

I was confused about two things, and it bothered me that they might be connected. The manzazu used some sort of power to reanimate the dead, and follow his bidding. It stood to reason that the more corpses he animated, the more power he used. Where was his power coming from?

The second thing that bothered me was the infants. The temple had taken infants from villages in Afghanistan, and our troops found mass burial sites with mummified infants. Here in Chesapeake there had been a rash of infants snatched up ever since the fake Abdul-Rayef had landed.

So, was the necromancer somehow using the babies to power his reanimation of the undead? That question was unsettling enough to make my stomach turn.

And getting back to the EMTs, if their stories were true, the manzazu had taken Delara's child, to force her to do his bidding. That's why I had been set up. The fact that the manzazu had used two living humans to shoot me was testament to my becoming a bigger pain in the ass than normal. He was upping his game. I didn't want to see his next escalation.

All those thoughts were swirling in my head when I finally found the LeMasters palace. I know that it wasn't actually a palace, but it certainly seemed like it. There was a high brick fence encircling the entire property, an electronic heavy duty gate at the entrance to the driveway, and a guard shack. A freaking guard shack! I glanced again at the fence. It wasn't a fence, it was a goddamn wall. Like the one in China. This place was a fortress.

I rolled my truck up to the entrance and put it in park, waiting for a guard to come out and ask me what I wanted. Looking in through the glass, I could see two of them, sitting in chairs. Time passed.

No one moved. I frowned. I was used to being ignored by women, but security types usually paid close attention to me. I waved. Nothing. I honked my horn. Still nothing.

I opened the door and got out. Sighing, I made a big show of slamming the door, making as much racket as I could. Still nothing stirred in the guard shack. I shook my head; it was impossible to get good help.

Suddenly I remembered why I was there. And what I was afraid of. This wasn't incompetence; it was bad news. My hand went to my hip, and I wrapped my fingers around the comforting grip of my Para.

Much more quietly, I crept to the door. I peeked inside through the glass. Both guards sat slumped in their chairs. It was hard to tell from the door, but it didn't seem like they were breathing.

Cautiously, I tried the knob. It turned. Gingerly, I opened the door and stepped partway into the room. "Excuse me," I said. That had an effect. Both guards shifted in their seats, their heads swiveling toward me. Both sets of eyes were burning an unholy red.

It freaked me out, but at the same time, I'd been expecting it. As they came to their feet and reached for me, I snatched my eight inch Ka-Bar from its sheath next to my 1911. I needed to keep this quiet. No sense warning everyone inside that I was here.

The undead made a concerted rush to grab me. What they lacked in finesse and technique they made up for in speed and grotesqueness. There was no hesitation at all, they just came for me.

I wanted to run out of the guard shack screaming. That wouldn't accomplish my mission, and it would have been a little bit awkward, me being a Force Recon Marine and all. So instead, I stepped completely into the room, kicked the door shut behind me, and sank my knife clean to the hilt in the right eye of the zombie closest to me.

The red glow faded out of the other eye, and the zombie fell to the floor without so much as a gurgle. This left me with one. Which shouldn't have been any sort of problem for a kick ass guy like myself.

Except that Murphy struck again. My knife was stuck in the first zombie's eye socket. Seriously, how often could one guy have the same problem, I asked myself, yanking at my blade, while I hunched my shoulder to keep the second zombie guard from fastening his hands on my throat.

You keep doing the same stupid shit, you're going to keep having the same stupid results, Bates informed me. Some help. He was the one that taught me how to use a knife in the first place.

The zombie growled at me, still trying to get a grip on my throat. I hit it with an elbow and growled back. I let go of my unhelpful knife and grabbed my opponent's head with both hands. One quick wrench later, the lights went out of its eyes, too, and it fell to the floor.

I got out of the shack as quickly as I could. Dead again or not, those bodies creeped me out. I debated going back in to open the gate, but decided against it. The gates opening and closing would give me away. The zombies probably weren't expecting company. I needed to preserve my stealth mode as long as possible.

Killing the guards and reanimating them, leaving them to attack me, showed that the manzazu totally expected me to show up. This was his way of giving me the finger, and telling me that it was too late. He knew that I'd be coming. I just didn't have to tell him exactly when. There still might be some advantage to staying covert.

Grabbing my rifle case from the floorboards of the truck, I pitched it over the wall by some trees. It took a bit to chin myself up to the top of the wall, since it was about eight feet tall, but I made it. I paused for a moment or two and used my vantage point to orient myself. I could see the house to the left, the huge garage ahead of me, a barn on the right, and the guest house between the barn and the garage. Between the house and the other buildings was a convoy of vehicles; several SUVs and a dark delivery truck that looked vaguely familiar.

I made a mental note to check out the barn first. I figured that I already knew what was in the other buildings. Enough stalling, I told myself. Time to go, Marine.

I took a deep breath and slipped over the wall.

CHAPTER 25

My feet hit the manicured lawn and I was boots on the ground in enemy territory. *No shit,* Bates sneered in my head. *What an idiot. If you're going to keep a running commentary in your head, can you at least be smart about it,* he said, heavy on the sarcasm.

I ignored him. It wasn't his life at stake out here. Picking up my rifle case, I unzipped it, pulled my AR-15 out, slammed a magazine home, yanked back the charging handle to rack a round, and looked at my immediate surroundings.

The lawn was immaculate and clear of debris. That was good. It was much less likely to have any hidden mines or other booby traps on an even, well maintained grass surface. I relaxed a little bit... then Bates spoke up again.

That doesn't mean that the yard isn't set with underground fence sensors, lamebrain. You may not get blown up, but you sure as hell will alert anyone watching monitors inside that you're out here, blundering around, he informed me.

"If that's the case," I whispered, "there's nothing that I can do about it. So I might as well just keep going." I have no idea why I was answering a voice in my head out loud. Maybe Sovers was right. I'd have to ask him if I survived to make my appointment later on.

In the meantime, I had ground to cover. I swept the case onto my back, clicked the safety off on the DPMS, and crept toward the barn. If you've ever seen a military group moving forward in a crouch, weapons up and ready, you've no doubt remarked on how cool it looked. Done in a group, it actually does look pretty cool. Done solo, you look like a jackass.

So there I was, moving across this perfect lawn, in bright sunshine, looking like a jackass. You learn to live with it. I already knew that the enemy was here. I had to find them, before they found me and rescue Colonel LeMasters. Then bury the manzazu, I growled to myself. Never forget that.

I reached the barn. The outside was just like the rest of the property; immaculate. It looked and smelled brand new and expensive. I avoided the big sliding main door, and tried a smaller side door. It was unlocked.

Cautiously, I pushed it open with the barrel of my AR. It swung silently in. I looked inside, and couldn't see anything in the gloom. It was quiet though, so I stepped in.

It appeared that I was in a central corridor or lane, or whatever people who had barns called the passageway right down the middle of their barn. I could see stalls on either side, with open doors. Apparently there were no animals housed here yet.

I frowned. It was quiet, and there was no animal smell, but I could smell something. Something...ripe. Or rotted. Like it was dead. Damn, I swore, and flicked on the light attached to my AR. I needed to see better.

Boy did I. The Streamlight bathed almost the entire barn with enough light to see clear into the corners. There were dead bodies everywhere. They were scattered around, in the stalls, in the corridor, up in the hayloft (as far as I knew), just laying around like they'd been dropped there; discarded playthings of a careless giant.

It didn't look like they'd been killed here; there was no blood anywhere, and no signs of violence. I also couldn't see any red glowing eyes. I relaxed just the slightest. No red eyes, no zombie.

Just to be thorough, I prodded the nearest one with the end of the rifle. I flipped it over. Red glaring eyes bored into my own shocked eyes. The body had been on its face, so that I couldn't see its eyes. I looked around quickly. If this one had been arranged that way, then maybe the others...

I brought my rifle up as fast as humanly possible. All around me, previously unmoving bodies were stirring, rising up in an obscene parody of the Resurrection. I'd been set up again. Like an idiot, I'd walked right into it.

With the need for stealth obviously gone, I opened up with the DPMS. That new red dot helped me immensely. In a target rich environment, I went from one zombie head to the next, pausing just long enough to fire once. In seconds, I was out of ammo, the bolt locking open on an empty magazine. There were bodies all around me, piled high and deep and unmoving.

But there were more. They were still coming, pouring out of stalls, clambering over their own fallen comrades, growling and reaching for me. I reached for another magazine on my tactical vest, and my hand closed on air. I wasn't wearing the tac vest from my days in the Corps; I had a rifle case slung across my back, and idiot that I am, I hadn't grabbed any other mags from it before I had moved out. Damn muscle memory.

I dropped the rifle on the ground in front of me and snatched out my Para Black Ops Recon. I was decent with a rifle, above average even for a Force Recon Marine, but my soul mate was this 1911. In spite of everything, I smiled as my hands came together around the grips of my double-stacked handgun.

At this point, I could probably have fought my way to the door and gotten out of the barn. I had the moxie, the space, and the weapon. I hadn't come here to retreat. "Retreat hell, I just got here!" was a famous Marine commander's battle cry, and I identified with that motto.

So I sidestepped to get around my AR on the ground, and went to work. My first two shots took two zombies straight in front of me out, and I pivoted right and dropped three more in less than two seconds. I jumped back to avoid one that was dropping at me from the ladder to the hayloft and took two shots to put out his lights.

Then I was grabbed from behind. I had jumped back right into another of the undead's embrace. Cold hands fastened onto my chest, and I could feel rotted teeth at my throat. Desperately, I whirled around, using the zombie's flailing legs to keep the others at bay. I hunched my shoulders as best I could, trying to keep the horrid mouth from finding my jugular.

I stuck the gun over my right shoulder and fired blindly at its head. It took three shots to make it let go, but it eventually did. Shuddering, I put one more into it while it was on the ground, and then swept the Para back up, ready and able to continue.

There were three of the undead coming at me all abreast, filling the entire width of the corridor. I shot each one once, grimly proud of my marksmanship, and then realized that the Para had locked open after the third shot. I was out. Fourteen rounds go fast during a zombie horde attack.

Luckily, I was almost out of enemies, at least for the time being. There were only two more of the ugly suckers stumbling after me. I dropped my empty mag, snagged a fresh one from my belt, and slammed it home. Reloaded, I took my time and drilled both with perfect shots low to the forehead, right between the eyes. They fell.

I stood panting in the middle of the barn surrounded, by literally heaps of bodies, in a cloud of gun smoke. I held my pose for almost an entire minute, making certain that nothing was moving. Deciding that it was clear, I holstered my sidearm and picked up my AR-15.

Having learned my lesson, I ejected the empty magazine, replaced it with a fresh one from the bag, and then took the other two from the bag and stuck them in thigh pouches on my tactical pants.

Having lost any semblance of covertness, I had to assume that my enemies would be waiting for me outside the barn. So I did what comes naturally to me: I kicked the door off of its hinges and burst outside, gun up and ready to rock and roll.

There was no one there. The yard was empty. That was it? The whole "army" that I'd been warned about was in the barn behind me, already dealt with? Maybe this manzazu guy wasn't so tough after all. I just needed to catch the little fucker. I looked at the house. Time for reckoning, I told the baddie. Here I come.

A movement to my right caught my peripheral vision. I turned my head, and there, throwing open the back doors to the delivery truck, was Delara. She looked my way briefly and then ran toward the house.

I let her go. Shooting zombies was one thing. Shooting enemy combatants, even, was fine for me. But there was no way I was shooting an unarmed woman. No way. Especially one that may not have been acting of her own free will. So I took my finger off of the trigger and pointed the muzzle at the sky and watched her run away.

Now what, I asked myself. The answer revealed itself almost immediately, as the eight-and-a-half-foot, four-hundred-pound Bengal tiger moved majestically out of the back of the delivery truck and dropped lightly onto the grass. Its head was up, and it was searching, sniffing the air. Its muscular tail swept back and forth angrily, and it slowly turned its face to where I was standing, foolishly out in the open, halfway between the barn and the garage.

It started moving slowly toward me, its stance low and menacing. I'd seen enough National Geographic specials to know that it was stalking me, in preparation for a leaping full on attack. Swell. I'd planned for zombies, an undead necromancer guy, and even possibly some human guards/military types, but a freaking tiger?

I pointed my AR-15 at it. The 5.56 round was not intended as a hunting round for even medium sized game, much less an apex predator. There was a good chance that I wouldn't even be able to stop this thing, unless I hit it with all thirty rounds. *Too bad your AR isn't full auto,* Lt. Rodriquez whispered. *You're gonna need them all. Good luck, Corporal.*

Thanks, I told him, with every bit of sarcasm I could muster. While I had been having my little internal conversation, the tiger had crept closer. He was fewer than twenty yards away now. He could probably spring that far in one bound.

I had nothing to gain by waiting. With a quick prayer thrown toward the God of Wayward Marines, I cut loose. My first three shots caught the huge feline off guard, and all three hit him clean in the side. I wasn't waiting around to see what damage any of my shots did, I was too busy pumping out more of them.

The tiger exploded into motion, jumping back and to the side after getting hit by hot lead running 3,300 feet per second. It roared and charged. I know that I hit it at least three or four more times, but it didn't seem to matter. The monstrous cat took two steps and then launched, soaring majestically high into the air and straight at me.

Normally, in an action movie, when the tiger leaps into the air, everything slows down to slow motion, and the world seems to just stop. Time stands still, and the hero gets that free time to pull whatever stunt the director and script writer have come up with. Real life doesn't work that way. That tiger jumped and in a blink, he was through the air and on me.

I'd been shooting the entire time, of course. You'd be surprised what a trained shooter can do in an eye blink, when sufficiently motivated. By the time the tiger landed, my gun locked back empty.

I'd held my ground, more out of terror than design, and the great cat had come straight in. The barrel of my AR-15 stabbed it in the center of its chest, and the entire four hundred pounds of cat slammed into me.

We hit the ground and I twisted, trying to get out from under the tiger, knowing that if he stayed on top of me I was dead. The beast flipped off to the side, rear legs kicking madly.

I rolled unsteadily to my feet, hands empty. The rifle was somewhere on the ground, empty. The cat stopped kicking and got to its feet. It had blood all over its side and chest, and wobbled on its paws, but it looked at me and snarled. Those five inch incisors promised me a really bad ending.

Not being a fan of that ending, and having a somewhat instinctive response to such threats, I fought back. I drew my handgun and started shooting as fast as I could. From less than five yards away, it's hard to miss with a .45. Four seconds and fourteen rounds later, I stood over the corpse of the Bengal tiger.

I had thought being in the barn, shooting all of those undead creatures was draining. Fighting and killing the tiger had wiped me out more than anything that I'd ever done. My arms and legs trembled uncontrollably. My hands twitched so badly that I dropped my gun on the ground.

Pick that up, Bates growled. *You might need it again soon. Pansy*, he taunted. Anything to get me to react the way he wanted me to. I understood, but wished that once in a while he'd try positive reinforcement.

Finally, after several long, deep breaths, I bent over and picked up the Para. I swapped out the empty magazine for a full one. That only left me one more. After that, I would have to use the Glock, and after that, I'd be reduced to harsh language.

Very carefully, I pulled the DPMS out from underneath the dead tiger. I wiped it off on a dry patch of fur and checked it. The AR seemed fine, so I dropped the empty mag and inserted another one. I'd gone through sixty rounds of 5.56, and twenty-eight rounds of .45 ACP, and hadn't even gotten to the house yet. At this rate, I was going need that harsh language.

I heard a sound. A door had closed at the house. How I heard it at all after all the gunfire was a mystery, but there was no doubt about it. Someone had just pulled a door closed. Which meant that someone had seen that I was still on my feet and more or less functional. Swell. Back to business.

No point at all in creeping. I might as well just march up to the door and walk in. I racked the DPMS and sauntered forward, feeling more stable and ready with each step. I saw a face in a window, staring out at me, eyes hidden behind dark sunglasses. I nodded at it, mentally promising it death when I got inside.

Without warning, the garage door was blasted outward, and a

Jeep Wrangler 4x4 came crashing at me, accelerating wildly. I threw myself to the side, diving out of the way just in time. The Jeep careened away, swerving and just barely missing the guest house and then the brick wall surrounding the property.

I got back to my feet and looked at the house. That face was still in the window, its attention on the Jeep. The features were hard to make out, especially with the sunglasses, but it looked familiar.

My attention got diverted again, as the Jeep came roaring back. Whoever was driving was by no means an expert, but they didn't need to be an expert to hit a big dumb Marine standing in the open with his mouth hanging open.

I chose fight over flight this time. As the Jeep spun its tires, tearing up the lawn, and came at me, I sent three rounds through the windshield and into the driver. When it continued coming at me, I gracefully sidestepped like a matador, and sent another round through the side window into the driver. To finish with a flourish, I spun and put two more rounds through the rear window and into the driver.

The Jeep lost speed. It drifted left, and came to a violent stop nose-first into a tree. The radiator burst, and steam hissed and billowed up. How Hollywood was that?, I asked myself. Like a damn movie. Maybe my friend Denzel had been right.

I waited, but no one came out of the wreck. I was pretty sure that whoever had been driving had been perforated multiple times, mostly in the head. So zombie or human henchman, that guy was toast. Enough was enough.

"Hey, you gutless bastard," I yelled at the house. "Enough of this shit. Come out and face me like a man, you fuckin' coward. Stop sending your undead clowns at me; they're not up to the task. Come on." I repeated, waving my AR at the house, motioning whoever was inside to come outside.

"Don't make me come inside and drag your ass out. Like Afghanistan," I taunted. I really was sick of this whole venture, and I was heartsick at the knowledge that my Colonel was most assuredly already dead. If nothing else, there was payback.

To my surprise, the front door opened. The inner door opened inward, and then, coming out through the screen door, was Colonel LeMasters, wearing dark sunglasses. Coming out behind him was a second man wearing sunglasses. Tucked into one arm was an infant. Held fast in his other hand was Delara, the Afghani receptionist. She too had an infant tucked in her free arm.

CHAPTER 26

I STOOD STARING AT THEM, my AR up and ready to fire. The group worked their way down the front steps and came to a stop not fifteen feet from me. The man between LeMasters and Delara readjusted the position of the infant in the crook of his elbow, and twisted Delara's arm to force her to a kneeling position in front of him.

The small woman was facing me, but kept her head down, avoiding my eyes. I didn't know if it was from shame, fear, or she was dead and had glowing red eyes. It couldn't matter to me. She had been helping the enemy. Maybe I couldn't shoot her, but I couldn't afford to work up any concern or sympathy for her, either. She wasn't my mission, the other captive was.

"Colonel? Are you okay?," I asked. "Sir, it's me; Corporal Brooks," I told him. "It's going to be okay. This shit show ends now," I growled to the figure in the middle. "You can take off the sunglasses, I know who you are. You're not Abdul-Rayef."

Without letting go of Delara, the man took off his sunglasses, and the twisted evil face that I'd seen in the temple before it'd blown up glared at me.

"Yeah, that's what I thought," I told him. "Do you even understand me, shithead?"

"I understand," he sneered, his voice low and as ugly as the expression on his face. "It is you who do not understand. You know nothing, worm. You are nothing more than a parasite, a minor inconvenience. I have sent only token minions to keep you chasing ghosts, or kill you if they could. Your continued survival is little more than a temporary problem."

I snorted in contempt and looked past him to the Colonel. "Say the word, sir, and this trash is history."

LeMasters didn't answer. I started to have a really bad feeling. "Sir?" I asked. "Say something, sir."

The Colonel's mouth opened. It stretched wide, but no sound emerged. After a moment, it closed again. Other than that, the man didn't move.

"Your master has nothing to say, worm," the manzazu hissed. "He is now under my control."

"Yeah, whatever," I muttered. I was unsure as to where to go next. I wanted to just shoot the son of a bitch, but I was worried about hitting the baby, and there was clearly something wrong with the Colonel.

"He's not my master, jerk. He's my commanding officer, and if you've done anything to him, you're going to pay dearly," I said, shifting subtly to get a better angle to take my shot. I tried again to get a response from LeMasters.

"Sir, say something. Anything," I implored. I glanced at Delara's face as she knelt, crouched protectively over the infant in her arm. A single tear ran down her face, and she slowly shook her head at me.

"Colonel," I tried, knowing that it wasn't going to have an effect.

The manzazu sneered. "I told you, worm; your master is now mine. You will be joining him soon enough, I think. It will be a pleasure to watch you move under my direction, your loyalty and obedience unquestioned."

"No thanks, I plan on living. The only way you get obedience is from dead people. Probably the only way you get laid, too," I snapped, and then looked at Delara. She was clutching the baby tighter yet, if that was possible. My eyes narrowed.

"Before I punch your lights out for good, tell me one thing: what is this sick obsession you have for babies? I mean, babies? What the hell?" I asked, not sure that I wanted an answer.

"These?" He asked, holding the infant in his grasp up in the air. "They are nothing. They are no more useful or important than batteries would be for you. They simply power my followers. When this one is used up, I will take another to drain," he sniffed.

I nodded. "That's the blackmail for Delara, then. You'll use her baby if she doesn't do what you want."

The manzazu waved his hand negligently, infant still clutched in his fingers. "I will take her offspring anyway. This one is close to being empty."

Delara looked up at me in horror. I'm certain that outcome had crossed her mind before, but hearing it stated so matter of factly was a shock. I stared back at her.

The manzazu was standing behind and just to the side of her, holding the infant in front of him to present me with a small sight picture. At fifteen feet, though, with an AR-15, it was still an easy shot.

Still looking at the kneeling woman, I pulled the trigger. My shot hit the necromancer in the face. His head snapped back and blood sprayed. I relaxed slightly, thinking that my problems were over.

Then the manzazu straightened and turned to face me again. Blood ran freely down past his jaw and down his neck. My shot had hit him in the cheek and then gone through his right ear. The eyes that had burned before with a black fury now glowed red. He released Delara from his grasp and pointed past me with a clawed hand.

"Now you die, worm," he cried. Delara gasped. She too was looking past me, at something behind me. I spun to see what had her attention. My heart dropped even further, as I watched the dead

Bengal tiger slowly come to its feet. It yawned spectacularly, showing every one of its fearsome teeth.

I almost lost it. Alive, the tiger had been almost too much for me and my pitiful armament. Dead, there was no way that I could put it down. Not that I had a choice. The zombie tiger crouched and sprang at me.

Despite my fear and the firm conviction that I was in over my head, my body still reacted like a trained warrior. The barrel of the DPMS swept the claws of the beast away as I shifted to my left. The big cat narrowly missed, and whirled to attack again.

At almost point blank range, I raked the cat's body with the 5.56, stitching new bloodless holes all over it. It didn't faze the tiger at all; it didn't even flinch from the multiple impacts.

Idiot, I told myself. Zombie cat. Head shots only. I tried again, this time aiming at the big skull of the feline, using the red eyes as targets. Several rounds whined off of the dense bone, tearing strips of fur away, but failing to penetrate and do any real damage.

Shit. Now what, I asked, fending off a fierce slash from a front paw. The tiger was now stalking me, taking random swipes with its claws. I backed away, fighting panic, and looking around for a miracle.

Hoping for the element of surprise, I yelled and charged the cat. Maybe in real life, like on one of those National Geographic specials, it would have worked. Cats are mysterious; no one really knows how they think.

This cat was not really a cat anymore, though. It was an undead creature, powered by the arcane abilities and thoughts of a necromancer. It did not react at all to my brave but foolhardy attack. It reared up and slapped me back with both giant paws.

I hit the ground hard, my body registering the impact and the sudden shocking pain of deep slashing cuts. The front of my shirt was shredded, and there was a lot of blood. I was in trouble. The cat waited, no doubt held in check by its sadistic master.

Painfully, I got back to my feet. It occurred to me that the problem wasn't actually the tiger; it was the power behind it. If I could cut the power, the cat would drop dead again. With that thought, I brought the AR-15 up as fast as I could and pointed it toward the manzazu. Long before I could get him in the sight picture and shoot, the tiger attacked.

I was forced to change my aim. I sent four rounds into the tiger's face. One incisor was shot away, and its cheeks looked mangled beyond recognition, but it didn't stop. I barely blocked the huge snapping jaws with the body of my rifle.

With a contemptuous growl, the zombie tiger tore the rifle from my hands and hurled it away. I heard the manzazu's voice again. "It's over, now, Marine. After you proved resourceful enough to beat my creations, and take out my idiot assassins, I decided to make use of the tiger to ensure my victory. This will be a fitting end," he gloated.

I reached for my Ka-Bar, determined to go down fighting. The undead beast opened its hideous mouth wide and leaped.

There was a deep roar from behind me and to my left. The top of the tiger's head lifted completely off of its skull and brain matter exploded in a mist. The undead animal collapsed in mid-spring, dropping unceremoniously in a heap at my feet. I looked at it in shock, and then pivoted slowly to my left rear.

"I told you that you needed this rifle, boy," Bill called. The old man was lying prone on top of the brick wall, with that gorgeous Wilson Combat 458 Socom stretched out in front of him. There were wisps of smoke coming from the end of the barrel.

My knees almost buckled in relief. That was a save from out of nowhere, I told myself. Who could have seen that one coming?

Bates mocked me. *Who indeed? Asshole. That old guy knew you couldn't do this by yourself. You just got bailed out by a guy that needs Metamucil just to shit.*

Who cares, I snapped back. The point is that he did rescue me. I'm still alive. It's time to end this.

I spun back toward the house, just in time to see the front door closing. LeMasters, Delara, and the manzazu were no longer in the yard. It wasn't over yet. I'd just had a major reprieve, but the damn necromancer was still out there.

I picked up my rifle, inserted my last mag, and looked over at Bill. He waved me toward the house.

"Go. Do your thing. I've got your six," he promised. "With your rifle," he added smugly. What a bastard.

I waved in acknowledgment and turned wearily toward the house. Now I had to play hide and seek with an Afghani sorcerer in a giant house that I'd never been in before. The odds were not in my favor.

Wait, my lieutenant told me. *You've never been in the house, true, but you have seen the layout. Remember?*

Pictures from the online magazine flooded my memory. A virtual tour played out, just as I'd seen it on my laptop. My eyes narrowed. I knew where they'd be.

I turned away from the house and ran to the garage. I skirted the wreckage of the destroyed door, and worked my way to the back. There was a workbench and a wall of tools, and a full-sized refrigerator along the back wall.

Crouching, I hid behind the refrigerator, the muzzle of my gun pointing straight at the wall of hanging screwdrivers and saws. I waited. Within three minutes, the wall swung out noiselessly on well-oiled hinges. I saw a hand, and then an arm, and then a head appear. It was Delara.

She was very cautious, looking all around the garage before stepping out. She saw me. The woman who had set me up and sent me to my death just a couple of days earlier stared at me with those haunted eyes. Time stood still.

Then she waved her arm, signaling all clear. She stepped into the garage, followed by the Colonel, still wearing his dark sunglasses, and finally, the manzazu. The sorcerer's injury was gone. His cheek and ear showed no damage at all, but there was still blood on his jaw and shirt.

He'd healed himself, most likely by siphoning energy from the infant that he still carried in his arms. I was going to have to separate him from his power source to beat him.

Instead of simply taking the shot, I leaned my rifle against the wall, stepped out from behind the refrigerator, and made a swipe at the baby he was carrying.

He was quicker than he looked, rolling his shoulder as he pivoted away to keep my hands off of the baby. I kicked his legs out from under him, sending him to the garage floor. I punched him once in the head, and grabbed for the baby again.

Strong hands seized my wrists, stopping me short of my goal. I looked over my shoulder in disbelief. Colonel LeMasters had me. There was no expression on his face.

I extended my hands out in front of me and at the same time shifted back one pace, ducking out from under the Colonel's arm, which broke his grip, and put me just behind him. He turned to find me, and I slapped him, hard, trying to break whatever hold the manzazu had over him.

The sunglasses flew from his face as his head rocked to the side. My heart froze in my chest as his head came back and his blazing red eyes bored into my soul. Colonel LeMasters was gone.

The undead creature that had once been my CO and friend grabbed me by the throat and slammed me sideways into the refrigerator. My head swam and I saw stars. The zombie stayed with its strategy and rammed me into the refrigerator again, with the same results.

It tried a third time, and this time I was able to thrust out with my left leg and plant it against the refrigerator door. I looked like I was doing a side kick to the refrigerator, but it worked.

From there I drove my right forearm into the zombie's left elbow, hard enough to break it. I followed through, freeing myself from its clutches for the moment.

Putting my left foot back on the floor, I grabbed my former commander's collar with both hands and pivoted hard left, slinging the zombie into the refrigerator.

"How do you like it?" I yelled. I bashed its head into the door over and over. I was messing up its face, but the door wasn't hard enough to do any real damage. I paused, looking for a better weapon.

The zombie took advantage of my inaction, and got inside of my arms and grabbed me in a bear hug. It lifted me up off the ground and pushed me up against the wall of the garage. I beat on its head, and tried to wrench it around enough to break its neck, but I didn't have the leverage.

The undead, following the commands of the necromancer, rocked back, taking me off of the wall, and then shoved me violently back into the wall again. I was getting really tired of getting smashed into things.

Up against the wall again for the moment, I felt around for something to use. My left hand found a hammer hanging on the wall from a hook. When the zombie pulled me away from the wall again, I brought the hammer with me.

Just as it was going to slam me back into the wall, I buried the claw end of the hammer deep into its skull. I watched the red light fade from its eyes, and the thing holding me became Colonel LeMasters dead again and nothing more.

We crashed to the floor together. I pushed my way out from underneath the corpse and staggered upright.

The manzazu was still in the garage with me. He stood facing me, one hand holding Delara by the throat, and his other hand holding her baby close. His sinister face was covered in sweat, but the gleam in his eyes was triumphant.

"You still lose, Marine. I will kill this woman as I did your Colonel, and then I will use her own offspring to command her to kill you," he gloated. It took me a minute to get my wind back enough to answer.

"Why not do it yourself, jerkoff?" I gasped. "Don't you ever do anything yourself? Just shoot me," I challenged him, holding my arms out to the sides.

"I do not sully myself with the likes of you, worm. What need have I of a firearm, when I command death itse..." I don't know what else he would have said, because in the middle of his speech I drew my Para and shot him in the middle of the forehead.

The manzazu's head snapped back again, as it had the last time I'd shot him. This time, though, I stepped up and snatched the baby out of his hands and shot him again. A third round, this time to the heart, dropped him to the garage floor.

Delara took her child from me and checked him over fearfully. I stood over the fallen sorcerer with my gun trained on his chest while she did that.

"How is..." I asked over my shoulder.

"I think he is okay," she called, hugging the baby tightly. "Jaleel is okay!"

"Good," I said, somewhat lamely. I prodded the body on the floor with my toe. It didn't move. I turned away and walked over to Delara.

"Come on, let's get out of here. It's over," I told her. I stopped and cocked my head. I heard noises. I knew that Bill was outside, watching and waiting, but it wasn't him making the noises.

There was the scraping sound of a foot being dragged the floor, coming from the secret passageway from the house to the garage. A woman with red eyes stumbled out, wearing a cocktail dress and a gaping red line across her throat. Mrs. LeMasters, who had been killed and then made into one of the undead. Behind her trailed two other shambling corpses in suits and combat boots. Bodyguards.

Why are they still on their feet, I asked myself. What the hell is going on?

They came toward me. I remained still, trying to sort out what was happening. As I hesitated, a fourth corpse stepped out from the tunnel. Red eyes glared out from the face of an eight-year-old girl, dressed in a smaller version of the same dress that her mother had died in. She opened a bloody mouth wide and came at me as well. It was too much.

I screamed in rage and emptied the entire rest of my magazine at them. The four bodies joined the rest on the floor. I looked down at the bodies of the Colonel James LeMasters and his wife and daughter. I knew that I hadn't killed them, not really, but it was my bullets that had torn up their bodies.

I turned to side and heaved, throwing up all over the only clear space left on the garage floor. Bent over, hands on my knees, I spit and then gasped, "I'm sorry," to Delara.

Straightening back up, I wiped my mouth with the back of my hand and looked over at indications of movement to my right. The body of the manzazu was shifting. Red gleamed from under its eyelids.

"Noooooo," Delara screamed, and opened up with the DPMS that I had left leaned against the wall behind the refrigerator. I covered my ears as she emptied the mag, holding the gun one handed, propped against her hip while her other arm cradled her son.

The bolt locked back, and the woman dropped the smoking gun. Taking a firmer grasp on Jaleel, she looked at me. "How did you know? I thought that you'd follow us into the house. The two bodyguards were set in ambush for you. The manzazu even had them holding their guns. I think that he could have made them use them. How did you know there was a tunnel?" She asked again.

"*Better Homes and Gardens*," I told her. I ignored her questioning look. It didn't matter, anyway. It was over. Most likely. I didn't want to assume anything, after the day that I'd had. I reached down and checked the body of the manzazu.

The damn thing moved again. Ripped almost into pieces, the body of the necromancer was still trying to fight. The Para appeared in my hands as if it had a mind of its own. I did a tactical mag change and then put every round into the manzazu, blowing the thing to hell where it belonged. When the smoke cleared, the manzazu was literally in pieces, and the other bodies were completely inert.

Crying uncontrollably, Delara threw herself against me. I held her, careful to not crush the baby, and trying to keep from falling down.

"Now what?" I asked. It was awkward just standing there,

holding a woman that I barely knew, and her child, surrounded by corpses. "We need to get out of here."

Delara resisted. "We need to burn the place down. Make sure that he is really destroyed, and so are all of his creations."

"I agree," Bill said, looking into the garage. "Burn it all down. And get the hell out, before the cops and who knows who else show up. You make a racket, boy," he accused, glaring at me.

I shrugged. Sometimes I'm eloquent as hell.

Delara groaned and burrowed in tighter against me, turning her head away from the carnage. "It isn't over," she whispered, pointing at the ground.

We looked at where she was pointing. The pieces of the manzazu were moving. The disembodied head was opening and closing its eyes, and a dismembered arm was slowly clenching and unclenching a clawed fist.

I made a move for my Glock, since both the DPMS and the Para were empty, but Bill put out a hand. "Wait. The other bodies aren't moving."

Looking around, I decided that he was right. Whatever evil power that thing had, there was still enough left that the parts of the manzazu had movement, but couldn't power anything else. Still... better safe than sorry. I nodded at a five gallon gas can sitting on the work bench.

Bill saw it and nodded as well. He reached into a pocket and pulled out a lighter. I decided that this wasn't the time to give him shit about his promise to his wife to quit smoking. Today I was glad that he hadn't.

Together we poured out gasoline from the five gallon can and another smaller can by the lawn mower. Delara stood off to the side, watching. She was still trembling. I figured that it would do her good to help with burning away the cause of her nightmares, too.

Yeah, McGavin snorted in my ear. *Chase Brooks, amateur psychologist. I guess if you can't be a kick ass Marine, you gotta do something.*

Go away, I told him. I cocked my head to the side, like a dog that senses something that puzzles it. Psychologist. That rings a bell, I told my old patrol buddy. Thanks.

I walked back into the garage. Bill asked me what the hell I was doing, and I just held up a finger. I'm not sure which one; but I was distracted. I found what I was looking for and stuck it into my rifle bag and zipped it closed.

Walking back out, I took Delara by the hand and brought her to the edge of the gas trail that Bill and I had poured. We stood there, looking down at the wet ground. Bill, grumpy old codger that he was, was still human enough to see what was going on. Without a word, he stepped up beside us and held the lighter out for Delara.

She let go of my hand, flicked the lighter open, thumbed the flint, and then paused, looking at the garage through the flickering flame. She looked at me. I held her gaze and then nodded.

She dropped the lighter onto the gasoline soaked driveway. The three of us stood silently and watched the flame work its way down the drive and into the garage. When the first crackling sounds started from within, and nothing came out of the garage at us, we turned as one and walked away.

True to form, Bill bitched about the gate still being closed.

EPILOGUE

I WAS a day late for my appointment, but I knew that Dr. Sovers would see me. He had too much to gain. When I walked into the reception room, the woman at the desk, always my biggest fan, grunted in disapproval and spoke into her headset.

Smiling quietly, I sat down in an empty chair without saying a word. The other four patients in the waiting room fidgeted nervously. I assumed that it was part of their underlying conditions, and why they were there. It probably wasn't because of me.

"Mr. Brooks, the doctor will see you shortly. Perhaps you would care for refreshment while you wait? There is a soda machine at the end of the hall on the fourth floor. I have correct change for you," the receptionist called out. I always knew she had a thing for me.

I smiled at her and shook my head. I was content to wait. Today would be worth it. She frowned and spoke into her headset again. She listened to whatever response there was, and rolled her eyes. She sighed dramatically and pointed at me. She curled her finger in a "come here" motion.

Obligingly, I rose from my seat in one motion, causing the guy nearest me to jump and start twitching. I walked to the front desk. "Yes, ma'am?"

"Mr. Brooks, you may go in. Stop at Sergeant Paxton's desk on your way," she told me. She seemed eager to send me on my way.

"You can call me Chase. We've been through so much together," I told her, my voice low and personal. She recoiled, and went back to typing without making any more eye contact.

I tried to keep my composure, but McGavin was laughing in my ear. *Ladykiller*, he giggled. *What a loser.*

"I am not a loser!" I yelled at McGavin, unfortunately out loud. The mental patients all flinched and stared at the floor. The receptionist froze. Carefully, she looked up.

"You are not a loser, Mr. Brooks. I have never heard anyone say that you were. We all have our problems, Mr. Brooks. You are fine," she said. "Go on in."

"Call me Chase," I reminded her and walked through the doorway to the looney bin, where Paxton was waiting. As always.

"Mr. Brooks," he breathed. "A day late. Probably more than a dollar short, as well. I hope you have a good excuse for missing your appointment yesterday. Dr. Sovers almost called the police. We know what you are, pal."

I said nothing, just stood staring at him. We stood toe to toe, engaged in a staring contest. Which was dumb on his part; I was at least six inches taller. I allowed myself a small smile.

Paxton scowled at me, knowing what I was thinking. "Well, asshole, let's see what you're trying to sneak in today. Or do you want to do it right, and put your arsenal in the tray yourself?"

I reached back and drew out my Para. Without breaking eye contact, I dropped the magazine, racked the slide to remove the round in the chamber, caught it in midair while still staring at Paxton, and put everything in the tray. I added a knife, and straightened up, standing at attention.

Paxton looked the tray and then up at me. "What about the gym bag, asshole? You're not going to see the doc with that. Put it down," he demanded.

I shifted the red gym bag on my shoulder to a more comfortable position and shook my head. "It's for the doc, not you. Relax, Paxton, it won't set off your metal detector. I promise. Now let me step through. By the way, I want my Sig P938 back when I come out from my appointment. I know you have it in the safe. You have no right to keep it."

Paxton sneered. "You aren't coming back this way after your appointment, smart ass. The doc is going to have you locked up, remember? That's why you pussied out of your appointment yesterday, right? You already know."

"You need a breath mint, Paxton. I will be back, you'll see. Tell you what: if I get committed, you can keep my little toy. If I come back, you open the safe and give me my firearm, along with my Para and my Emerson folder. Sound good?" I asked. "Good, I'll see you soon," I promised, and sauntered off down the hallway.

Dr. Sovers opened the door himself when I knocked. He looked tense. I smiled. It didn't help. I smiled a little wider. Still didn't help. I gave up and walked into his office and sat down.

Sovers walked carefully around me and sat behind his desk. Once behind his throne, he seemed to gain composure. He clasped his hands on the desk and leaned forward. This time I didn't lean away. He frowned again and seemed to hesitate.

Finally, as I sat silent and still, he spoke. "Mr. Brooks. Do you remember our last meeting? I informed you that on the occasion of your next visit, you would be remanded to our psych ward for a stay of not less than forty-eight hours, and probably longer, and we would try to help you with your delusions? I assume that you do in fact remember it, and that it was the reason for your no-show yesterday."

"I do." Of course. I'm not stupid.

"Then you must have come today knowing that you were going to stay with us for a time, Mr. Brooks. Did you bring clothes and a few personal items in that gym bag?" Sovers asked, smiling for the first time.

"No." Gym bag is for you, I told him silently.

"Mr. Brooks; Chase...you must understand that it's in your best interest. Especially in light of Colonel LeMasters' unfortunate passing just the other day. We only want you to be strong enough to face the truth, and then go about your life, healthy. That's why we are going to keep you here for a time," he told me, smiling condescendingly. He reached in his desk for something, and then pulled out some papers to place on the desk between us.

"Here, Mr. Brooks, are the forms that we just need to fill out. I have a pen," he offered, reaching into his suit pocket.

"Actually," I interrupted, taking the gym bag back off of my shoulder. "Actually, if *you* remember correctly, doctor, we had a deal. At the end of our last session, it was agreed that you were going to keep me in at the nuthouse unless I could provide proof of the undead creatures that kept attacking me. Do you remember that?"

Sovers stared at me, trying to get a measure of what I was leading to. Finally, he bit the bullet. "Yes, Mr. Brooks, I do remember that. You agreed to submit to an extended stay at this facility failing your ability to demonstrate the absolute proof of your claims of the undead being out to get you," he said. It wasn't quite the way it had gone down, but it was enough. I had my moment.

Without a word, I unzipped the bag, reached in and set the severed arm of the manzazu in the middle of my unbelieving doctor's desk. The hand, fingers ending in black claws, twitched and began dragging the arm across the desk.

I stood and left the office without saying a word. Dr. Sovers sat, staring at the crawling hand, and remained mute.

At the guard station, I stared in superior fashion at Paxton, reloading my Para and slipping it back in its holster, stashing my folder my front pocket, and with much relish, chambering a round into my Sig P938 and settling it in the ankle holster that I'd worn to the hospital. I could hear his teeth grinding from clear across the room.